FLORA NWAPA

ONE IS ENOUGH

Africa World Press, Inc.

P.O. Box 1892
Trenton, New Jersey 08607

Africa World Press, Inc.

P. O. Box 1892
Trenton, NJ 08607

First published in Nigeria by TANA PRESS 1986
First Africa World Press edition 1992
Second printing 1995

Cover design and illustration by Ife Designs

ISBN: 0-86543-322-4   Cloth
        0-86543-323-2   Paper

ABOUT THE AUTHOR

Flora Nwapa is Nigeria's first woman novelist, author of the highly praised *Efuru, Idu, This is Lagos and Other Stories, Never Again, Wives at War* and *Women are Different*.

All the characters in this collection are imaginary and bear no resemblance to anyone alive or dead.

For all women of the world, I repeat an Hausa proverb: A woman who holds her husband as a father, dies an orphan.

Chapter 1

It was six in the morning when Amaka knocked at the door of her mother-in-law's room. She asked Amaka to come in as if she'd been expecting her. Amaka was not sure what her offence was but her mother-in-law had been so rude to her the night before that she'd been unable to sleep.

So, at six in the morning, she had decided to apologise to her mother-in-law, for what she did not quite know.

'Mother, forgive me,' she heard herself saying. 'It will not happen again. I should not have replied to what you said. I am very sorry, Mother. Please, don't throw me away, Mother.'

That expression 'don't throw me away' was not the expression of her people. She would have said 'reject', but she did not want to use that word, it was too painful. Throw away was better. But Amaka was not the type to be rejected or even, as she said, to be thrown away. She had made her mark in business. She was a woman to be reckoned with. Why should she be pleading in this way, and humiliating herself this morning? But she wanted peace. And, besides, she wanted to remain married to her husband, who was a loving husband.

Amaka had always wanted to be married. She envied married people, and when at last Obiora decided to marry her, she was on top of the world. She was going to show everybody that a woman's ambition was marriage, a home that she could call her own, a man she would love and cherish, and children to crown the marriage. Although things had not worked out as she had hoped, she was desperately anxious to preserve her marriage.

There was a knock at the door, and her husband came in and sat on the bed. Did he know she was there? Amaka had not told him that she was coming to see his mother. Why was he there? Did he always visit his mother in the early hours of the morning and she did not know?

'What is she saying to you?' Obiora asked, and the question hit Amaka in the face. It was as if a heavy blow had landed on her forehead. Was that her husband talking or a stranger? That was not her husband's voice, the husband who never in their six years of marriage had said an unkind word to her.

'What are you saying to my mother?' He directed the question, this time, to Amaka.

'I was asking her to forgive me, not to throw me away,' Amaka heard herself saying.

'What have you done?' he asked. There was silence. That was it, that was the crux of the matter – what had she done?

'You see, I don't understand this nonsense. I just do not understand why . . .'

'Will you shut up and let your wife talk!' shouted Obiora's mother. 'She has come to see me. Allow her to say what she has come to say. Who asked you to come here anyway? Please remove yourself from my room. Now, my son's wife, tell me why you have come to see me this morning. Just sit down there,' and she felt the side of the bed and motioned her to sit down. 'Don't kneel any more, get up and sit here.'

Obiora left the room and the two women were alone. Amaka swallowed hard. She had planned what she wanted to say before she came in, now she was at a loss as to what to say next. And she was tired, she couldn't help yawning. Her mother-in-law moved from the bed, and encouraged her to go on.

'Go on and tell me, why are you yawning this early morning? Didn't you have a good sleep?'

2

'I slept badly, Mother.'

'So did I. I have been sleeping badly for the past year. Don't you see how thin I am? Was I as thin as this when you married my son six years ago? So don't complain of sleeping badly for just one night. Now go on and say why you are here.'

'Oh, my God!' exclaimed Amaka. 'It's getting more and more difficult. Mother,' she finally went on. 'You have known my plight. It's not my fault and . . . '

'It's my son's fault then,' the mother said.

'I didn't say it was your son's fault either. It is fate. Fate is playing tricks on me. Fate is unkind to me.'

'And so my son should suffer, should continue to suffer because of your ill-luck, because of your stubbornness, because of your stupidity, because of your . . .'

'I am not saying so. I merely . . .'

'Merely saying what?' she asked with a kind of contempt that was like a stab in Amaka's heart.

'All I am saying is that you should give me time. I have another place to go. The place was recommended by a friend of mine who has recently returned from overseas. We shall go next week. I hear that the doctor never fails. He has been highly recommended by this friend of mine. I understand that his father was a great native gynaecologist.

'This doctor was interested in his father's profession and therefore read medicine in Russia, so as to complement the medicine he learnt from his own father with that of the white people. So, next week we shall go to Benin. The doctor is from there. That's what I have come to tell you. Please bear with me and all will be well.'

When she finished, there was no response from the older woman. Amaka was surprised at herself. That was not what she had come to say to her mother-in-law. There was in fact no such doctor that she knew. What was happening to her? Why did this kind of story come to her at this crucial time?

3

Was she begging for time? She had been told by many gynaecologists that there was no likelihood of her ever becoming pregnant. There was something wrong with her tubes. She had asked sensible and intelligent questions, and received almost identical answers from the medical men she had visited.

Inside her, there was this faith, this blind faith that all the gynaecologists she had seen were wrong, and that she, in God's good time, would have a baby, no, babies. This feeling, this faith, never left her. She kept saying to herself over and over again in moments of emotional instability, 'I will have babies. The doctors are all wrong. I will have babies, boys and girls.' She saw babies in her dreams. She was given both baby boys and baby girls in her dreams by unknown people. She did not reject them. She took them, cleaned them and put them in babycots to sleep. She would then wake up to find that it was a dream. She would weep, her husband would hear her weeping, come to her room and wipe her tears and tell her that as she believed and had faith that they would be blessed with children, so did he too believe. Then she would feel better.

However, things had begun to change a few months back when there was still no sign of pregnancy. Her husband became short-tempered, and almost inattentive. He began to undergo a change, and Amaka noticed it all, but chose not to discuss it, saying that if she was pregnant, everything would be back to normal.

Amaka went on with her business in Onitsha, supplying timber, sand and food. She was a contractor, one of the numerous female contractors who had sprung up during and at the end of the war. Before the war, she had been a teacher. At the end of the war, because she took part in the 'attack trade', she rediscovered herself. She was amazed at what she was able to do and to accomplish. She and other women went right behind the enemy lines and bought from the

4

enemy who were killing their people. There was nothing else they could do. They had to eat and have other bare necessities like toilet soap, toilet rolls, cigarettes and all the other things which Biafra could ill afford during the war.

She made money, but had no child, and her husband had been patient these six years. Was she going to behave like other women, and deceive her husband? Tell him that she was pregnant, then after a reasonable amount of time say that she had miscarried? Was she going to do that? She could fool her husband, but not her mother-in-law. The old woman was determined. She used to be friendly, now she was not. What had she in her mind? What was her plan? Was there a girl somewhere for her husband? Amaka even asked her husband to go anywhere and have a baby but he did not welcome the idea. Perhaps his mother had convinced him to look elsewhere.

When Obiora's mother began to talk, Amaka could not believe her ears. 'My son's wife, you are a liar. You are a miserable and poor liar. I am sorry for you. Now listen to me carefully for I have had enough of your nonsense for a long time. Why are you apologising to me? I don't need any apology. You think you are clever. I am cleverer than you are and all your friends who come here, eat my son's food and talk ill of him behind his back.

'And you, with your ilk talk of my son, my lovely son, my good son who saved you from shame and from humiliation. How many suitors had you before my son came to marry you? I told him not to marry you. I shouted it from the rooftops. I told Obiora not to marry you, that you were going to be barren. But he would not listen to me. I begged my two daughters, and even my young son, to beg Obiora not to marry you, but he refused all my entreaties. He disobeyed me and he married you.'

Shocked and confused, Amaka's mind raced to her very first suitor, Obi. He was a very nice man and had come from

5

a very good home. Amaka's mother was fond of him and encouraged the relationship. The understanding that both families would be in-laws had been fully established when news came to Amaka's mother that the young man had married another girl in church.

Amaka went hysterical. For days she did not eat. The rejection took her a long time to overcome. What was wrong with her? Why did the young man not keep his promise? Her mother was always by her side. She told her not to worry. She was still young and all would be well. 'You just have to forget the man. He was not for you. If he were for you, then he would not have married someone else. Count yourself lucky that it happened now and not after the marriage. It would have been much worse.'

Amaka tried hard and began to look at her plight philosophically. Perhaps it was God's will. Perhaps someone much better would come along. Oh, she wanted to be married and have children. Her sole ambition was to be a wife and mother. If she achieved this, then all the blessings of this world would come in God's good time. So she waited.

Then came her beloved one, Isaac was his name. Isaac made Amaka know what being in love meant. Isaac taught her to enjoy sex. Hitherto she had believed that sex was what a man and a woman did to have babies. The pleasure part of it was unknown to her.

Isaac, for his own part, was surprised at Amaka's innocence and ignorance. The questions Amaka asked intrigued him. They were innocent sixteen-year-old questions. What intrigued Isaac more, was that Amaka was genuinely eager to learn. In bed they were in bliss, in heaven. They talked, they were able to communicate both in body and in soul. They both enjoyed their sex life as well as the little talks in between.

But then in spite of all, Isaac would not propose. And Amaka waited. Being shy by nature, she did not want to

6

bring up the matter. If Isaac was unmarried, and he seemed to love her so much, why did he not propose? Two people who loved each other so much should go ahead and consummate their love in marriage.

A year passed and there was no proposal. Amaka was not getting any younger. In fact people had started throwing in hints here and there, and they embarrassed her. But she loved Isaac. She wanted to be with him always. She did not play games. She was a oneman woman. She could not manage having affairs with several men at the same time. Her friends told her that she was making a mistake. There was nothing that was certain except death. But Amaka could not change her nature. Then tragedy struck. Amaka was preparing the evening meal when a friend rushed in, wanting to say something but restraining herself. Amaka was suspicious.

'Tell me that Isaac is dead,' she said quietly.

Her friend stared at her, tears in her eyes.

'Go ahead and tell me that Isaac is dead. Say it.'

The friend said, 'I'm sorry, Amaka, Isaac is dead. He died in a motor accident along Enugu-Okigwe road. His body is in the mortuary in Enugu.'

Amaka's friend took her hand and she followed like a woman possessed. They sat down on the bed and wept together. Then she wiped away her tears and stared into space.

'What is fate doing to me, Obiageli? What have I done?'

But her friend said nothing. She was the one who had urged her to have as many men friends as possible, because one never knew what was in stock for one. It would be cruel to remind her friend of this, so she kept quiet. Amaka did not blame anyone. She only blamed fate.

When she was trying to recover from the death of Isaac, she met her third man, Bob. Bob was a playboy. A week after their meeting, Bob proposed. Amaka was sceptical. She neither said yes nor no. It worried her. Then she decided to talk to her aunt. When she told her, she shook her head. 'No, my daughter, I don't like him. I know his family well. He is not going to be a good husband. I heard he did not care for his mother. His mother was very old, and he was an only child, and they said he would not even send money to her, let alone get a maid for her. When his mother got a little girl to take care of her, he came home on leave, pounced on this girl and made her pregnant. The mother said, well, that was what I wanted, that was what I had planned, now marry her.

'And do you know what he did? He told the girl to abort the pregnancy. The girl was afraid and ran to her mother. That girl is married now, a loss to Bob's mother. Then Bob and his mother went to the girl's parents and demanded the child, because it was a boy. Of course, the girl's parents did not listen to them.

'And that's the man who wants to marry you. No, my sister's daughter. Let's wait for a while. A good man will come. But, let me make it clear to you. Please don't bottle yourself up. You are not going to be in a nunnery. What is important is not marriage as such, but children, being able to have children, being a mother. A marriage is no marriage without children. Have your children, be able to look after them, and you will be respected.

'I married a man I did not like. And in spite of the fact that I have my children, I have neither respect nor regard for my husband. You can see that, can't you? He is the father of all my children all right, but from the day I was betrothed to him I disliked him. When I had seven children in seven years of marriage, I knew I had had enough, and stopped sleeping with my husband. Of course, he protested. He reported it to my mother, but I would not budge. No more. I had tolerated him for seven years. He had given me seven children. What else did I want from him?

'When he began making too much fuss about this, I got a

sixteen year old girl for him. Yes, I married her for him. I said to her, this is our husband, take care of him. I am going to take care of our children. I must see that they all have a good education. Good education means money. So I am concentrating on my children and my business.

'That was how I turned my back on my husband. He became prosperous, and married more wives. I was the head wife and was expected to do my duties. These I did. Now my children are all grown. All have got married and are living in different parts of Nigeria. My daughters have rich husbands. I planned all the marriages. They are happy with their husbands, but I say to them, never depend on your husband. Never slave for him. Have your own business no matter how small, because you never can tell. Above all, I told them, never leave your husbands. I did not leave mine, but I was independent of him. If I did not take this line of action, I would not have given my children the basic education I was able to give them.

'Marriage can make and unmake one. I learnt a lot from my own mother and I am putting into practice what she taught me. It has worked well for me and my children. It will work for you as well. But you are too simple and too trusting. You seem not to know what you want in life. Come out of your shell. Come nearer to me. You are my sister's daughter, perhaps I have been too busy and have neglected you. Whatever it is, there is going to be a change today. You have come to me about Bob. You will not marry him.'

Amaka was left as confused as ever. Bob tried to get her interested in him, but was unsuccessful. She was not going to marry just for the sake of marrying. Marriage was her goal at all times, all right, but she had to bide her time.

Yet, she was uncomfortable. Her age-grades were all getting married and leaving home. They were all having children and playing mother roles that Amaka envied and cherished. Was she going to be left on the shelf? Attending age-grade functions those days was a great ordeal. She could not live down the cruel allusions to the fact that she had not found a suitor. Some of her age-grades, either to make fun of her or out of sympathy for her plight, made clumsy match-making attempts which embarrassed and angered her.

One of them had suggested a divorced man with five children. Amaka did not mind the children. What she minded was the status of the man, and his ugliness. Had things really gone so far that her own friends could think of such a man as her husband? Did having a husband mean that kind of comedown? For Amaka was ambitious. She wanted to excel in everything, and beat all her sisters and her friends and age-grades. In spite of her misfortunes, her head was held high. If she did not marry well like her sisters, she would excel in other things. She would be in business, she would make money and her sisters, friends and age-grades would respect her.

Then another tragedy struck. Bob was killed. Amaka was shocked and afraid. What was going on? she asked herself several times. She felt nothing for Bob of course, but then he and Isaac had died tragically, and they both had something to do with her. They both wanted at one time or another to marry her.

There was something mysterious working against her or for her. If she had married Isaac, she would have been a widow and if she had married Bob, the same fate would have befallen her. There was definitely a force behind it all. This mysterious force was working for her, not against her. She should therefore be thankful to God that she was saved twice from being a widow.

In spite of all these misfortunes, Amaka was doing marvellously well in her business. Soon she bought a plot of land and began planning a house of her own. Her mother welcomed this move. And she it was who encouraged her to go on. 'The richer you are,' she told her, 'the better your husband will be and he will really appreciate you. Your husband's relatives will appreciate you as well. But, remember, make men friends and start thinking of having children. Marriage or no marriage, have children. Your children will take care of you in your old age. You will be very lonely then if you don't have children. As a mother, you are fulfilled.'

How awkward for Amaka. That was not what she learnt in her few years at school. The good missionaries had emphasised chastity, marriage and the home. Her mother was teaching something different. Was it something traditional which she did not know because she went to school and was taught the tradition of the white missionaries?

How was she to make the approach? How was she to get pregnant without a husband? What was she going to say to her married friends, to her age-grades, to her business associates? And what was more, who would look after the business while she became pregnant?

Her mother dismissed all these questions with a wave of the hand. 'What were you taught in that school of yours? Plan, plan, plan, what are you planning for? Did I sit down and say, I am going to have seven children, three boys and four girls and no more?

'You create problems where there are none. Let yourself go, I say. Are you a child? Tell me, how old are you and how old am I? When I gave birth to you, I must have been twenty-seven or twenty-eight. Now tell me, what is the difference in our ages, that I have to teach you what to do to have a worthy life? I say look at me and learn from me, you fool.'

It was after this encounter with her mother that Amaka met her future husband, Obiora. Although he came from her area, Obiora had lived in the North so she had never met him until he transferred to Onitsha as an executive officer in one of the Ministries in which a girl friend of Amaka's, Adaobi, also worked. Through Adaobi, Amaka met Obiora and was instantly attracted to him. He was quiet and gentle in manner and behaviour and Amaka felt she could trust and depend on him. Obiora made it clear to everyone that he admired Amaka and was interested in marrying her, and all concerned thought it was an ideal match. Amaka did not feel as intensely as she had with Isaac but she was sure Obiora would make a much better husband. The courtship lasted for about six months and they were married in church in Onitsha after completing the traditional marriage ceremonies.

Six years later, there was no child. Obiora's mother was tired of waiting, and so she had come to a final solution. Obiora must have an heir, because his brothers and sisters all had heirs.

Chapter 2

Obiora's mother continued:

'Tell me, my son's wife, since you married my son, six years ago, how many times have I visited your home? Go ahead and tell me how many times.' And she paused so that Amaka could reply, but Amaka said nothing.

'Well, since you cannot answer me, I will tell you. This is the sixth time I have visited you.' Amaka swallowed, and shifted her position, and said to herself: 'Well, I asked for this. Six times indeed!'

'Did you hear me?' her mother-in-law continued.

'Yes, Mother, I heard you. You said you had visited six times since we were married six years ago. I can hear you very well, Mother.'

'Whether you hear or not, it will end today. Everything will end today when I finish with you. The hold you have on my son will end today. Do you hear me? I have waited for six years, and I cannot wait for even one day more. Didn't you see how I hushed up Obiora when he came in to interfere? He is a stupid son. Sometimes I wonder whether he is my son. But I know he takes after his useless father, making a lot of fuss without backing his fuss with action. If my son heard me, if he listened to me, his house would have been full of children by now.

'Let me take your points one by one. You said you saw a doctor, or are about to see a doctor who could treat you and make you pregnant. I say you are a liar. All the doctors you saw said that you were incapable of bearing a child. You were dishonest not to tell your husband that he was wasting his strength on you. I know your mother very well. Do you think that if she had had no child in her husband's place that she would stay? She is a woman I admire very much. We have a lot in common. But I should have thought that she would have come to me so that we would put our heads together and plan what to do. Well, she thought she was clever. I am going to tell her that I am cleverer. She was blessed and I was not. Maybe that was what she meant by keeping quiet all these years. I am surprised at her. She was the only one I considered when my son wanted to marry you. But it did seem as if she had changed or that she had become wicked. Tell me, you said I knew your plight. What is your plight? You are barren. That's all, barren. A year or so ago, you said you had a miscarriage. My son came to tell me. I laughed at him. I did not let him know that you were deceiving him. So, my son's wife, you were never pregnant. and you never will be. Get that clear in your mind. I have been told this by many native doctors and some of the doctors you have visited as I mentioned earlier.

'Yesterday, when I talked to you and you flared up, didn't you see how I watched you? I watched you and sized you up and saw that you were a big fool. Didn't you see how I hushed up my son this morning? I hushed him up too last night, and stopped him from striking you because he wanted to strike you when you flared up. I thought they said that those who went to school did not get angry easily, that they controlled their temper, unlike us who did not see the inside of a classroom nor bore the teachers' whips. My son has two sons and tomorrow the mother of these sons will come and live in this house with her sons. We have performed all the ceremonies, and she is coming . . .'

At this, Amaka was utterly shocked. She began to tremble. She could no longer control her emotions. She held on to the bed, so she did not faint. Obiora has two sons by another woman. And he never told her? Impossible. How

14

could he do that to me? She was brought back to herself by her mother-in-law's words.

'My son's wife and mother of his sons wanted you thrown out of this house. But I told her I would have none of it, that you will not be thrown out because you are the first wife. I too am the first wife of my husband. So I told her categorically that you would not be thrown out.

'Obiora, my son, was surprised at me. I said to him, "Why are you surprised? I am not unkind to your wife. Other mothers would have thrown her out, not me. Amaka's mother, if she were in my shoes, would have thrown her out, not me. That's me. I am fair, and there is nobody fairer than I am in this community of ours."

'That's why I keep telling you that you are very foolish, that you didn't know who your friends or enemies were. You went to school, and you have this business that is making little money so you think you know everything. You know absolutely nothing.

'The next thing I want to tell you is that you have done nothing at all towards the advancement of my son since you married him six years ago. Look around and you see others married at the time you were married. My son has not started building a house yet, nor has he done anything for his age-grade in this town.

'And look at you, looking younger and younger every day while my son is getting older and older every day. You and Uzoka's daughter got married at the same time. Her husband and my son belong to the same age-grade, they started working the same year. Look at him now, he has built himself a house. He has changed his car twice since then. But you and my son will continue to drive the car he bought two years after his marriage to you . . . and . . .'

Amaka no longer listened. It was she who bought the car and presented it to her husband. One thing she begged of him was that he should not say that she bought it. It was the

15

second year of their marriage and Obiora's Volkswagen had 'knocked engine' and there was no money to send it in for repairs. So Amaka asked about the price of a Peugeot, went to the bank, withdrew all the money she had and gave it to her husband, and told him to go and buy a Peugeot 504. Her husband could not believe it. He was so proud of her. He told his friends when they came to see the car that his good wife had bought it.

Amaka intervened and told their friends that Obiora was just being modest, and that in fact his rich mother had bought the car for them. When the guests left, Obiora asked her the meaning of the lie. All she said was that she did not want anybody to know that she bought the car. She felt that people might look down on him.

'But you bought it, Amaka. I am proud of you. I am proud I married you. My God, how many men can boast of wives presenting them with the raw cash to buy a Peugeot 504? Just tell me.'

'I know, darling. I know, but I don't want people to know. Let's keep it to ourselves, please.'

What then was her mother-in-law talking about? But for her, Obiora would have been fired from the Ministry because of his carelessness and over-trusting nature. She it was who went to his Permanent Secretary in Enugu and told him all she knew about her husband's involvement in the whole matter. So her husband, rather than losing a year's seniority, was merely reprimanded. Others who were involved lost their jobs, benefits and gratuities. Many wives bore her a grudge because she was able to help her husband while they were not.

And what was her husband's mother talking about looking younger while her husband aged? Was she responsible for that as well? For all she knew, she fed her husband three times a day. What she gave her husband was what she ate. And she was always at home, no matter how

16

busy she was, to have a meal with her husband.

But then she knew that in the society in which they lived, particularly in her own community, a wife took the blame for her husband's failure in business or in life generally. In the good old days, a wife also took the praise for her husband's success in life. Alas, it was no longer so, for the pattern of life was changing. A husband was content if his wife got rich by dint of hard work or good fortune. He relaxed and let his wife spoil him. He bragged to his age-grade: 'If you want to know a good wife and how a man should be treated, just consult my wife.'

Times changed, and men began to assert their masculinity over their industrious wives. Men made fun of husbands, at drinking places and functions, whose wives were well-to-do, saying: 'Look at him, just take a good look at him. He is less than a man, depending on a woman to buy his shirts for him, to spread out the mat for him. One day, instead of him, forking her, she will fork him.' And they spat to show their disgust.

Amaka longed for the good old days, but then could not see herself ever going the whole hog. For instance, her mother-in-law would be right if she suggested that Amaka should marry a wife for her husband now that it was confirmed that she was barren. She herself would take care of the young girl and the children when they began to arrive. But she could not bring herself to do that just then because of the changes and pattern of live in that society. Amaka suddenly realised that her mother-in-law had stopped speaking, and was looking at her angrily.

'Mother, I am sorry,' she said. 'You have told me many things which I must think about. Let us talk again tomorrow.'

Quickly Amaka got off the bed and ran out of the room before her mother-in-law could reply.

Chapter 3

Obiora's mother went away later in the morning without another word with Amaka. Obiora in turn looked unhappy and when Amaka asked why he was so unhappy, he hushed her up.

'What does my being happy or unhappy mean to you? Why won't you leave me in peace? You want me to bare my heart to you. You'd want me to tell you how my heart beats if I knew how. Woman, enough is enough. I am going to work.'

'What about Mother? She hasn't taken anything. I didn't see any of her clothes in her room. How come she has taken her leave so unceremoniously?'

'This is her home and she can come and go as she thinks fit, so don't let that worry you. She will be back again soon.'

'Obiora, she said certain things to me which made no sense to me. Why did you never tell me you had taken another wife?'

Obiora looked uncomfortable. 'I have just married her recently.'

'But you have two children by her.'

'Yes. Well, what was I to do? Remain childless because my wife is barren?'

'Why didn't you talk to me about it?'

'Because I knew you'd oppose me and react just like you're doing now.'

'Should I not react, for God's sake! What do you think I am made of – wood?'

There was an awkward silence, then Amaka went on: 'All

18

right, leaving that for one moment, why did you not tell her about the car? You should have told her that I purchased the car with my hard-earned money for our comfort, but especially for your comfort. I thought you could have told her that if nothing else. I did not want to mention my intervention in the Ministry because that was not concrete enough. Anybody could claim that he helped you out of your trouble. But I was particularly upset about the car. If we must wash our dirty linen in public, we must not hide anything. All our underwear should be publicly washed in the open and I mean it.'

'You might as well say that you fed me since you married me,' Obiora said weakly.

'Not exactly,' Amaka replied. 'No, it would be untrue if I said that. But I complemented the food budget. That I did and you know it. Tell me how much did you give me for food? Go and ask other wives and they will tell you how much your colleagues in the same Ministry give their wives. But I did not grumble, I never asked for more. Perhaps that was my mistake, not asking for more . . .'

'You are being senseless,' burst out Obiora. 'How many mouths were we feeding? You barren and senseless woman! You forget that you are childless. You would not raise your voice in this house if you were sensible. You should go about your business quietly and not offend anyone because if you do, one would be tempted to give you one or two home truths. I warned you several times when you got pregnant during our first year of marriage, but you were careless and lost the baby. It was your fault.

'I have made my decision and there is no going back. What Mother told you will happen, not today but soon. So brace yourself for a hard time. If you are sensible, you will stay here under my protection. A woman needs protection from her husband. If you want to act as if you are endowed with all the wisdom of Solomon, and get wrong and stupid advice, all

19

well and good. You are at liberty to do exactly what you want to do.

'But let me warn you that if you step out of this house in protest when my wife and my two sons arrive, you stay out forever. You must not come back. I am not the type of man to go begging with cap in hand for you to come back. I have outgrown that. So watch your next step and be well advised. Out of the goodness of my heart, I am asking you to stay. But if you choose to leave your matrimonial home, here is the door.' Saying this, Obiora stormed out through the same door.

Amaka remained where she was like a statue. That was not her husband talking to her. That was a strange voice inside her husband. There was a demon, or rather demons talking through her husband. What Christ said about demons in the New Testament was correct. When a man was out of balance, it meant that evil sprits had entered the man, and had played havoc with him. No, that voice was not her husband's voice, Obiora's voice.

But Amaka was not going to lose her head, far from it. She would watch events. She believed in marriage. Marriage had sobered her, had made her tolerant and peaceful. Only her fate played pranks. God had deprived her of the greatest blessing bestowed on a woman, the joy of being a mother.

Was that really the end of the world? Was she useless to society if she were not a mother? Was she useless to the world if she were unmarried? Surely not. Why then was she suffering these indignities both from her husband and his mother? She could adopt a son and a daughter. She could play mother to them. She would go to a distant place, maybe Ghana or even Zaire and adopt a boy and a girl.

These faraway places appealed to her. The children would grow up not knowing their relatives, and even when they found out that they were not her own children, they could not trace their home. She would do this. She would love them and they would love her.

Then she thought of the children of her brothers and sisters. She could ask them to send over a child each. She would look after them. They would call her auntie and she would love them, send them to school and really pet them. That was better than adoption. She was still very conservative. She did not fancy the idea of adoption. What about the genetic danger? No, she would rather ask for some of her nieces and nephews. She would do that. They were her flesh and blood.

Yet another thought. She could marry a young girl and push her on to her husband. She would dress the girl well so she would be attractive to her husband. Her husband would sleep with her, and she would become pregnant. As soon as she was pregnant, she would take her away from her husband and take care of her. She would take her to the hospital to make sure, then she would confine her to the house until she had the baby.

Then what happened after she had had the baby? Would she be able to control her? She shrugged her shoulders. She did not want to control anyone. She wanted just to be. She wanted peace to go about her business, look beautiful, wear good clothes, go to the hairdresser every week, in fact, enjoy life fully.

No, she was not going to marry a wife and push her on to her husband. She was merely going to get a maid and allow the maid to please herself and if she became pregnant, claim the baby as her own. Again the same problem arose, the genetic one. Just anyone would not do.

'What a life!' Amaka exclaimed. She thought of her youthful days. Perhaps it was destined that she would not be married, least of all have children. Why then was she wasting her time staying at Obiora's as his wife when she knew beyond all reasonable doubt that the marriage had broken

21

down? A native doctor she had visited at one time in Lagos had told her that marriage would continue to elude her. He advised her not to marry. When Amaka asked whether she could have children without marriage, the native doctor was honest in saying that he was not sure. He had examined her, and had called a woman from his own cult to examine her. The woman made a thorough examination and told her that she would bear fruit, but she needed a special man to make her do so.

Amaka was angry and stormed out of the place. She had heard before she made the visit that the people of that cult in Lagos committed sexual offences including incest. So when the native woman doctor said what she said, Amaka's back was up. She thought that the next step would be for the native doctor himself or someone around to make advances. No, she wanted children, but not as desperately as that.

Her thoughts wandered – was she useless to the world because she was childless? Was she unfulfilled because she had no child? Her mind went to the good missionaries who taught her in her young days. They chose to be in the service of God rather than having a family. Were they unfulfilled as well? Should they not in their old age be happy to hear about the boys and girls they taught and nurtured as ministers and heads of state in their countries? Did they not have the contentment that they had done God's work on earth and merited the kingdom of God?

Was a woman nothing because she was unmarried or barren? Was there no other fulfilment for her? Could she not be happy, in the real sense of the word, just by having men friends who were not husbands? There did seem to be some magic about the word 'husband'. Her people had drummed it into their ears as children growing up that a girl just had one ambition – to be married. So all energy was geared towards finding her a good husband.

But Amaka knew from the behaviour of her illiterate aunt

22

and mother that they did not share in this belief of her people. Her mother brought them up to be independent, but she did not emphasise marriage. She had several children no doubt, but her emphasis was on self-determination and motherhood. She lacked the guts to ask her formidable mother how she was going to have the children without being married.

Amaka wondered how her married sisters were getting on in their matrimonial homes. They had been brought up to despise their father because he was of no consequence. He had too many wives and he was a drunkard. He was of no use to them when they needed him most, and when he died, it was more or less a relief for them. It was good riddance, and they almost celebrated his passing away. Their mother was at her best. She so demonstrated her grief that she nearly convinced her people that she cared for her late husband. But she did not care. All her children knew that she did not care. The boys especially knew, and it hurt them so much that they put up feeble fights in support of their father, but they did not succeed. In the end, their mother won them over.

What was Amaka going to do if she decided to leave her husband? How was she going to cope? Men would seek her all right, but would they not make fun of her? Would they not use her, and when they were tired of her, discard her? There was a lot to be said for marriage, for a man one was able to rely on and cherish and all that. But when there was no such man, what should a woman do? Create the man? Take second best? Live alone, have another woman as they now do in Europe and America? Or what?

One thing was certain now, after the fight with Obiora. She would leave and set up house somewhere. She would live a single and respected life. No one would point an accusing finger at her and call her a whore as her husband often had. She would find fulfilment, she would find pleasure, even happiness in being a single woman. The erroneous belief that without a husband a woman was nothing must be disproved.

Amaka felt exhausted. She forced herself to go about her business listlessly that day, not really knowing what she was doing. She made terrible mistakes, and snapped at the man who tried to correct her.

'You have overpaid me,' the man said.

'That's your luck. Leave me alone,' Amaka snapped.

'You have overpaid me by one hundred naira, do you hear me? Has something come over you? Are you well?'

'What did you say?' Amaka finally asked. It was dawning on her what the good man was saying.

'You have overpaid me by one hundred naira.'

'Oh, my God. Is that so? Thank you, my good man. I don't feel good today. Please pardon me.'

Amaka left the site after this incident and went straight home. The maid was there. Her husband had returned home, eaten and gone out. She managed to eat something and went to her room to rest. She was just about to fall asleep, when her husband returned.

'You were not in when I returned,' he began.

She wanted to say to him: 'How many times this week did you meet me at home when you returned from work?' But she thought better of it and said nothing.

'Have you seen my mother?' he asked.

'I have not seen your mother. Did she come back?'

'She told you she would come back today. I hope you have prepared some food for her. As you know, she is very particular about what she eats.'

'The maid will take care of that. We have everything in the house,' she said.

'I don't want the maid to cook it. I want you to do the cooking yourself for my mother. If you don't want to cook it, I will have to do it myself or get someone to do it for me.'

'Perhaps you can get someone to do it for you. I am tired.

24

In fact, I am exhausted. I can hardly get up from this bed. Just do exactly as you wish and leave me alone, I beg you.'

'Did you say I should do as I wish?'

'I said that. You have been doing as you wish for quite some time now. There is no one to stop you from pleasing yourself. What I want you to do for me is to simply leave me alone. I repeat, leave me alone.'

There was silence. Then Obiora said: 'Have you seen them?'

'Seen whom?' Amaka replied.

'My sons,' he said.

'No, I have not seen them. Where are they?'

'My mother brought them here in the morning. You were at your site.'

'Where are they now?'

'My mother must have taken them away again,' he said.

'I am glad for you. I am happy for you,' she said.

'Are you happy?' he asked suspiciously.

'Of course I am.' 'You are not just pretending to be happy?'

'I am happy and sad as well. Happy because you have proof of your manhood. Sad because I cannot have a baby, and your proof is also the proof of my barrenness.'

'How you talk. It is not as bad as that,' he said.

'It is worse than all that. Let's not go into it any further. You have not answered my question. Where is the mother of your sons now?'

'You mean my wife?'

'Whatever you choose to call her. I will continue to call her the mother of your sons. Where is she?'

'You will call her my wife. She is my wife,' he said.

'Congratulations. I thought that in this sort of thing a wife, even a barren one, should have been taken into confidence. It beats me how you should do all this behind my back, be involved with a woman, have sons by her, marry her without breathing a word to your wife. You have changed a good deal, my husband. I too could change, you know.'

'Meaning what?'

'Meaning that I could do a lot behind your back without your ever finding out,' she said.

'Like prostitution?'

'No. God forbid, our land forbids that. Our gods and goddesses forbid it. Our women, we women of our land abhor it. I abhor it particularly not only for moral reasons, but because I was never cut out to be that. I could never make love to two men at the same time for money, or out of what they call love.'

'Go on, you haven't said anything that I haven't heard from you. What would you do behind my back?'

'Nothing.'

'Nothing?'

'Yes, nothing. I won't be a prostitute, that's all I know.'

'What then? Sleep around with other men? Out with it. What would you do behind my back?'

'What have you been doing behind my back?'

'I am a man.'

'I am a woman.'

He rushed at her. He was a very strong man. He had beaten her once during their six years of marriage and she did not recover from that beating for a week. Her face was swollen, her head ached. She had bruises all over her. Obiora was sorry and contrite. For one week also he did not go to work. He took sick leave and stayed with her. He cooked for her, he was genuinely sorry. He doted on her and told her that it would never happen again. That was the second year of their marriage. The fire of love was still burning high. She could not actually remember what provoked that beating. There was an argument, she refused to yield, because she was sure of what she was saying. And he refused to yield because he was her husband and by virtue of that, he was right. You did not argue with your husband. A woman who tried to win an argument over her husband was regarded as a 'he' woman.

Amaka refused to give in. She could be stubborn, so she pressed on. Then to stop all argument, to stop his wife lording it over him, he used brute force. He beat her so mercilessly that Amaka was afraid that he was going to kill her. She raised the alarm, and by the time neighbours gathered, Obiora had taken her in his arms and was weeping himself and he begged his neighbours to leave them alone.

Amaka learnt one thing from that incident and it was that she would never helplessly watch a man, least of all her husband, beat her. She must defend herself. She arrived at this conclusion herself. So when she went to the hairdresser's one Saturday and heard a newly married girl narrate how her husband beat her up so badly that she fainted and was rushed to hospital, where she remained for two weeks, she said to her:

'He will do it again. Men are beasts, so watch out. Think of what it was that led to the beating and make sure that this trouble does not repeat itself. If your husband was a good man, he would try to avoid that problem. But the trouble with our men is their ego. They refuse to appreciate their wives. Mind you, they do apreciate their mothers and sisters, but never their wives. Your husband will always show you that he is a man, and put you in your rightful place which is under his thumb. Your rightful place is not in the kitchen as we erroneously think, but right under his thumb. He would like to control your every movement, and it is worse if you depend on him financially.

'But regarding the beating, be ready at all times to defend yourself. Never cry out when he is beating you, without finding something to retaliate. So I say, fight back. Get a stick nearby. If he lands a blow on your face, get the stick and land a blow on his body. But I must warn you, never on his

27

head or you might kill him. I once heard of a man who went about parading himself as a philosopher and an academic. He had a beautiful but senseless wife, so the story went, as if beauty and sense did not go together. This academic cum philosopher for no just cause beat up his wife so mercilessly that this senseless beauty learnt her lesson fast. A day came when there was another fight. Before he pounced on her like a bull-fighter, she had this heavy iron rod which she landed on the man's back. The man was on the floor and wept like a child. She called in an ambulance and the husband was taken to hospital. He was there for three months. Dare he beat his wife again?'

Obiora never beat her again after that incident, and she in her own way tried to avoid any argument that could lead to a show of strength, to the proof of who was actually wearing the trousers in their relationship. Why then was Obiora rushing at her now to beat her? No, she was not going to fight him. It was too late in the day. A lot had happened in the past year. Her husband had undergone so much change. Fighting now was useless. She wanted to keep up the marriage. She did not want to leave him. But it did seem to her that there was a conspiracy to provoke her so that she would leave her matrimonial home.

For one thing, when Obiora told her that he had sons, she was not happy, but she was relieved. She felt peace within her. At least her husband was happy. People now knew that the fault was hers and not his. It could be painful, this realisation, but it was soothing as well, to Amaka who was loving and sweet in her own way.

Therefore she did not fight back. She did what she had never done before. She ran from her husband, dashing into the toilet and locking the door.

Obiora banged on the door. 'Open the door, you whore, you good-for-nothing woman, you prostitute. What have you been doing behind my back? Sleeping with other men? I am going to kill you today and take your corpse to your mother, and nobody will ask questions. You mean you have been sleeping with men in our matrimonial bed? Is that what you mean? Open the door and I will tear you to pieces.'

Amaka looked round the small toilet. She was really frightened now, but also very angry at such violent aggression. There was a hammer which the carpenter had used to mend the door of the toilet a day before. God bless the carpenter, he forgot to take his hammer. Nigerian craftsmen and their attitude to work! How come that a carpenter could forget his most important tool, a hammer, and for a day he hadn't missed it?

She armed herself with the hammer, and waited. At first, she wanted to open the door and attack her husband, but she changed her mind. Doing so would be aggression. She would wait for her husband to break the door down then attack him with the hammer – that would be self-defence.

Would the door not break? Amaka thought as her husband banged away. It must have been a strong door after all, resisting all that force.

Then, all of a sudden, without warning, the door was open. Amaka dodged as her husband came after her bare-handed. Then she sprang up quickly and landed a heavy blow on her husband's chest with the hammer. He simply sprawled down on the toilet floor, unable even to cry out.

'I have killed him, I have killed him! Obiora, Obiora, please talk to me. Have I killed you? Oh, my God, have I killed you? Please say something, say something to Amaka, your wife. Come, come I have killed my husband, I have killed him. Come, everybody, come, call the police, I have killed him. Don't you hear me, my people? I have killed him. Here is the carpenter's hammer, that's the evidence. I used it, I gave him a blow, I have killed him. He did nothing to me. I am a bad woman. Come, all of you, come to save him and kill me.'

Neighbours gathered around, all ears and eyes agog at the dramatic scene. Then the 'queen mother' sailed in, saw the crowd and fainted. Both mother and son were rushed to the hospital by kindly neighbours.

Chapter 4

Once she had satisfied herself that Obiora was suffering more from shock than any severe injury, Amaka decided to leave her marital home. It was obvious that her marriage was dead and the sooner it was buried the better. Since she had decided to leave the house it was better to move far away, out of Onitsha altogether. But where? Who did she have outside Onitsha? Why, her sister, Ayo, of course, who had recently moved to Lagos and had been asking her to come there for a holiday. Well, Lagos it would be. Lagos was the place for business, to make money and live well.

In twenty-four hours, Amaka had packed her personal belongings into a large trunk which she left with her mother. After a few weeks she took one suitcase of clothes with her on the bus to Lagos. Her sister was delighted to see her. The next day Amaka went into town to shop for some basic necessities for herself.

Amaka was shopping in Kingsway Stores, Lagos, when she saw Adaobi. They recognised each other at once. 'Amaka, welcome to Lagos. How are you, my dear?' And they embraced once again. Adaobi then took Amaka to the coffee shop.

'Are you here for a holiday? Where are you staying? How's Obiora?' Adaobi fired questions at Amaka as they sat down and ordered drinks.

'Give me a chance, my dear. I have a long story to tell you.'

When Amaka finished recounting her experiences, Adaobi was silent for few minutes. Then she reflected slowly, 'Ego told me a bit of what happened to you and your marriage. I cannot imagine the whole incident. Obiora was such a lovely person. So considerate and loving. How can he have changed so much?'

Adaobi and Obiora had been friendly in school. Obiora was very fond of Adaobi and wanted to marry her, but Adaobi was not keen. Obiora's mother was not keen either. It was in the company of Adaobi that Obiora met Amaka and fell for her.

'It's my luck,' Amaka said. 'When I left my marital home, my mother was upset. I was greeted with harsh words. You know my mother. Let me tell you what my mother said to me. "You fool," she said to me. "You are not my daughter. I told you to leave that husband of yours years ago if he was unable to make you pregnant." Adaobi, you know how crude she is. She went on and on. She was so merciless, so cruel that I burst into tears. But she did not stop, she went on. "I told you, four years ago, to leave him, or if you did not want to leave him, to go to other men and get pregnant. You are my daughter. We are never barren in our family, never. Even in your own imbecile father's family, there was nothing like barrenness. But you refused to take my advice. You were being a good wife, chastity, faithfulness my foot. You can go ahead and eat virtue. Here are your belongings sent to me in this disgraceful manner, my daughter, humiliated in this way. You are not my daughter. Did you now witness what happened when your eldest sister's husband started fooling around? I gave my daughter advice, and she took it. Her husband came to me. He came all the way from Jos to beg me to forgive him. I forgave him and warned him.

' "You had the guts to tell me in the presence of your husband not to interfere in the affairs of your home. Shit! What do you mean by interference? Why should I not have a say about the happiness of my daughter and her husband? If I did not interfere, then I was wicked. I had failed in my duty as a mother.

32

' "Then your other sister came up with the superior attitude of one who went to the home of the white men. I gave her one or two home truths when her dandy husband got himself a mistress old enough to be his mother. I told her what to do. She did it. Her husband called a truce. His position was threatened. He did not want to lose his job because of the gossip that would have ensued if he had been foolish enough to throw his wife out.

' "Ayo is the only one among you who is like me. She took no nonsense from any man. When her husband came up with his pranks, she left him and got herself 'kept' by a Permanent Secretary whose wife went to the land of the white people to read books. Foolish woman, to leave her husband for that length of time to read books.

' "Ayo moved in. In four years, she had four children. In four years her 'husband' had sent her to school to improve. She is cleverer than all of you. She qualified as a teacher. In the fifth year she was able to make her 'husband' buy her a house in Surulere, and that year the wife returned without anything, and my daughter moved out gracefully with her children, into her own home.

' "In her position, what does she want from a man? I want to ask you. Now when it is almost too late in life, you come crying to me. Shame on you." Then she began to weep. I have never seen my mother weep in that way before. When our father died, she did not weep like that. That weeping and my suffering must have changed me a good deal. I stayed with her for a while, then decided to come to Lagos to start life again.'

'Never mind, Amaka. I am happy to see you in Lagos,' said Adaobi. 'I have always said and believed that if one makes a mistake in marriage one should not live with one's mistake. One should try and start again. I know you well and what you are capable of doing.'

'Right now, in spite of everything, I still love Obiora. I

thought, erroneously at first, that marriage involved two people. I thought the emphasis was on this unique relationship of man and woman, that children did not even matter. I was wrong. A childless marriage cannot last in the Nigeria of today. So if a wife is unable to have children by her husband, she should leave and try elsewhere.'

They ordered more coffee and soft drinks. 'Adaobi,' Amaka went on. 'I am confused. I am a motherly person. I need just one man. I am not like my sister. But now, the idea of a husband scares me. I have come to Lagos to start afresh. I did contract work at Onitsha. I can do it here if I can find someone to help me.'

'I shall talk to my husband. Perhaps he can help. Cheer up and don't wear your misfortune on your face. You never know, things might turn out well for you now that you have changed location.'

The women talked of their schooldays and their friends. Those who had made it and those who were not so lucky. One particular girl was remembered. Each time Amaka remembered her story, she admired her courage.

This girl was three years their senior, very energetic and brilliant. In her last year in school, she became pregnant. The man responsible was in a top position in government. His wife had died suddenly in a motor accident, and this girl, Tunde, together with some neighbours had rallied round for the funeral and all that.

This man fancied Tunde, and the result was that she became pregnant. Tunde went to him and told him. He asked her what she intended to do. She said she wanted to have the baby. 'You will have the baby, and I am responsible,' the man said. So Tunde carried her baby. She hoped that no one would discover. She was only eighteen. She showed no sign of change or tiredness or weakness. She did what was expected of her. She took part in games as usual and did her school work very well.

But then, how could one hide pregnancy? It began to show. The girls gossiped and the teachers heard. She was summoned to the principal's office. She denied she was pregnant. The school doctor was called in and he confirmed that she was five months pregnant. She could deny no more. The man responsible came to the principal and owned up to his responsibility. He would marry her, he was sorry, it was a mistake, he said. But he was talking to the wind. Neither the principal nor the teachers or even the girls sympathised with Tunde and her lover.

So she was sent down but was allowed to take her exams. The girls were unkind to her. They made fun of her, and she was miserable.

The school authorities did not stop at that. A very elderly mother was invited to the school to talk to the girls about the merits of virginity. Their virginity was sacred. It was their pride. It was valuable. It was respected by their husbands, and if it was lost, it could never be regained.

Adaobi was determined to help her friend Amaka. When she got home that afternoon she told her husband about her.

'Mike, you remember that girl I used to tell you about in our class who seemed to have everything?'

'Yes, what happened to her?'

'She is in Lagos. I met her in the Kingsway Stores today and she told me about her marriage.'

'The one you encouraged your boyfriend to marry?'

'If you want to put it that way.'

'Your boyfriend, Obiora. I saved you from that man, Adaobi.'

'You did, my darling husband. Don't I show how grateful I am to you for saving me from the wicked boyfriend? You did, my love. There is no denying it. But Obiora has changed a good deal. He used to be such a wonderful lover, so considerate, so understanding. There was never a dull moment when you were with him. I was madly in love with him in those days. Then Papa said no to our marriage. Then Papa convinced Mama, and there was nothing I could do.'

'That was when I came in. You were being difficult. You brought up all sorts of problems, but I did not budge, because the moment I saw you when I returned home on leave, I knew I had found a wife. I did not leave a stone unturned to make you mine. I did everything possible to make you say yes.

'Your mother and father were agreeable all right, but they raised the religious problem. They nearly got me on that, but I told them I was prepared to have a mixed marriage. My mother protested, but I calmed her down. I knew that your grandparents were instrumental in the founding of the Anglican church in your town, and that the church was regarded as your grandparents' property. It would therefore not be proper for you to abandon the church. I knew what I was doing. If you had followed my religion at that time, the influence of your church in your town would have diminished.'

'Then after doing what you were supposed to do, you refused to go to my church, except on ceremonial occasions.'

'Tell me, was it easy for you to follow our Mass?' asked Mike.

'It wasn't,' she said truthfully.

'There you are. I was brought up to be a Roman Catholic. It wasn't easy for me to change. But I tried.'

'Okay, you win.'

Then one of their children came in.

'Mommy, were you arguing with Daddy? I heard your voice. What is the argument about?' It was their third child, who was only three and a half.

'No, my angel, we were not arguing,' and they began to laugh. 'Have you had your milk, Adaeze?' Adaobi asked.

'Mommy, I don't drink milk any more. Only Obi drinks milk. Only babies drink milk, Mommy, and I am not a baby.

Obi is the baby of the house. I am a big girl and . . .'

She ran out of the bedroom when she heard her nanny call her.

'Adaeze is another one,' Mike said. 'The way she grows. At this rate she will be taller than our first one before she is ten. I think she takes after your father, who is six foot one. But she is a woman. She should not be too tall.'

'You sound like a male chauvinist. What has height got to do with our Adaeze?'

'A lot, my feminist wife. Who will marry her if she becomes five foot eleven? She would need a giant of a man to cope.'

'What's wrong with a woman marrying a man who is shorter than her, I want to know?'

'I don't really know, but it has always been so.'

'And it could never be otherwise. Therefore we should try and retard our daughter's fast growth.'

'If there was anything I could do to do that, I would do it,' said her husband.

'So she marries someone taller than herself. In their time, I don't think they will put up with what their mothers put up with,' Adaobi said.

'She will remain single then, a miserable spinster, left on the shelf. I suppose you would love that.'

'Oh, she could have men friends, have children and live an independent life,' she said.

'And who is stuffing your head with these unnatural ideas. What have you been reading? Yes, you said you saw your former boyfriend's wife. What did she say to you?'

Adaobi was sensible. She had gone too far. She did not want to go on with the conversation. So it was a welcome relief when her husband asked about Amaka and what she had said to her.

'Amaka has left Obiora in very painful circumstances. You know she has been unable to have a child. She didn't

37

want to leave really, but things came to a head and she had to leave. She is in Lagos now and wants to start doing contract work here. So I thought you might help. I saw her in Kingsway Stores. She said a lot to me. Darling, when one sees people like Amaka, one thanks God for small mercies.'

'Has she registered her company?' he asked.

'I think she has, but I will ask her. She will come to see us on Sunday.'

Amaka was at her friend's house on Sunday. Adaobi's husband was in and welcomed her with an open heart. Amaka was rather sensitive these days but she liked the way she was welcomed and was pleased.

'You have a beautiful home. I like your garden, so well kept.'

'That's your friend's handiwork. I am rarely at home. How she finds the time to cook, garden, take care of the children, attend church meetings and work full-time beats my imagination. She is a wonderful wife and a wonderful mother.'

Amaka was envious of her friend Adaobi. Some people were meant to enjoy while others were born to suffer. She saw in her friend's marriage what she had planned for herself. But it was not to be. It was fate. Some people were lucky and some were not so lucky. All those who asked her hand in marriage before Obiora finally married her were not for her. She had come to Lagos to have a clean break with her past. She had come to start life again at the age of thirty, when some of her friends who married early were becoming grandmothers.

Adaobi's husband brought her some soft drinks and persuaded her to have a shandy with him. She agreed and the shandy, beer and fanta orange, did not taste bad at all.

'Adaobi told me you were now in Lagos and wanted to do some contract jobs,' he began.

'Oh, yes,' Amaka replied. She was a bit taken aback by

38

Adaobi's husband's informality but she rather appreciated it.

'Mike, please come here for a minute,' called Adaobi.

He rushed to the kitchen to the aid of his wife. Then he quickly came back. 'I have been telling your friend she works too hard. She won't listen. She is so fastidious. She has maids and servants in that boy's quarters, but she chooses to do everything herself. The one thing I put a stop to was pounding yam. And she talks of male chauvinism and all that. One day she will become ill and not know the cause. So do talk to her.'

Amaka was impressed. So there were husbands who cared for their wives. Adaobi was a lucky woman, blessed with such a husband and children.

'You will have to register your company in Lagos,' Mike said.

'I have already registered my company,' she said.

'That's good. You are already in business. Have you your registration papers with you?'

She had them. 'That's very good,' Mike said. Then Adaobi came and announced that lunch was served and they moved to the dining room. They were about to start eating when the steward announced that Rev. Fr. Mclaid was at the door. Adaobi went to the door and brought in the august visitor.

'Father, you always meet us well as they say. Please sit here. Meet my friend Mrs. Amaka Iheto. Rev. Fr. Mclaid,' she said to Amaka. They shook hands and the man of God sat down and ate with them.

He did not take his eyes off Amaka. He stared at her, and made poor company. Amaka was conscious that she was being closely observed and was embarrassed. Fortunately, Mike was talking away, and Adaobi was busy playing the good hostess that she was, so she noticed nothing.

'How is your parish, Father? You are so busy these days. Last Sunday at Mass I asked about you and was told you went to the East. How was the East? The young lady here, a good friend of my wife's, is from the East, Onitsha in fact. Since the war ended. I have not been there. I am scared. I saw the war, the ravages of war, and when it ended, I was among the first group to return to Lagos. God bless Gowon. Since then I have refused to go home. My mother is not happy with me, nor my father either. Yet I don't feel like going home at all. I send them pocket money from time to time and remain here. Adaobi has nagged and nagged, but has given up.

Fr. Mclaid smiled and said, 'Never mind. You will go one day to bury your mother or your father. Thank God I have no parents to bury. Have you taken out insurance for that, Mike and Adaobi?'

'For what?' Adaobi asked, placing another dish of soup on the table. It was piping hot and Amaka was enjoying the meal very much. It was cooked that day. Her sister cooked only on Sundays, got the soups frozen, and did not cook again until the next Sunday.

Mike heard the Father all right but chose not to answer. 'Well, I think one should write about the high cost of dying these days. I tell you, I am glad that I don't have any parents to bury. If I had, I would have to break into a bank and rob it of all it has. Our people spend a fortune to send the dead to their ancestors.

'You know what a friend said the other day,' the Father continued. 'He said he had instructed his wife to bury him in Lagos when he dies. A very jovial person. But the wife did not take it kindly so she came to me in tears. I told her not to worry, that it would be all right, that her husband did not mean what he said. She insisted that he meant it. That was not the first time he had said it to her. Did it mean that since he had worked as a civil servant, he could not afford a decent burial at home?'

They laughed. 'But tell me, Father, don't you have uncles? Your father's brothers, your mother's brothers? You know how clannish our people are. When any of them dies, they will pounce on you.'

'Are you from the East?' Amaka asked the Father. That was her first direct remark to him.

'Father is somewhere from the East,' Mike said, happy to change the subject.

'Why the name then?' Amaka asked.

'It is a long story,' Mike said, and the Father grinned.

Chapter 5

Amaka was ready before five in the morning to go to the Ministry to see a friend of her brother-in-law who had asked her to come and see her. 'Wait until it is at least five thirty,' her sister said, surprised that she was ready to go to Lagos. 'And, besides, you have to eat something. Have some tea or coffee and bread, please. And, Amaka, you have to take it easy in Lagos.' That was Amaka's sister, Ayo, who lived in Surulere with her children.

Amaka chose to go to the Ministry early so that she would see the man. So she set out. She walked for a good ten minutes before she got to the bus stop. She could not struggle to get a seat in any of the buses. She waited and waited, but could get no transport. Just when she had made up her mind that she would take a taxi if one came along, a car stopped, and the driver asked her where she was going. 'Lagos,' she said. 'Get in,' he said and opened the door for her.

Amaka sat down and the man drove away. Amaka was not afraid. She had lived in Lagos. She spoke a bit of Lagos Yoruba. She knew her way about. So she relaxed and waited for whatever the man was about to say or do.

But, to her surprise, the man said nothing to her. He simply drove on and on and Amaka became worried. This was unlike Lagos. In the good old days before the war, when a man stopped to give you a lift and you accepted, you immediately got acquainted and chatted away as if you had known each other for years. Why was this man not saying anything to her? She must start a conversation.

'It is kind of you to give me a lift, sir. I am grateful to you,' she said.

'Oh, the pleasure is mine,' the man said. There was an awkward five minute silence. Amaka was getting uncomfortable now. Was the man taking her somewhere to kill her? There were so many cases of murder in Lagos. Children had disappeared, wives and husbands had left for work and had not returned to their homes, and there were no traces of them, not even their bodies.

The traffic was slow. It was not quite seven in the morning. They were moving towards Lagos all right. Lagos had changed a good deal, but Amaka still knew her way around. She thought of something to say to the man, but came up with nothing.

Then the man spoke: 'What part of Lagos are you going to?' he asked.

'Broad Street,' she replied, relieved.

'You mean Yakubu Gowon Street?' he said and smiled for the first time.

'Oh, is that what they call the street now?' Amaka said, feeling comfortable now.

'Yes, after the name of our Head of State. The street was changed from Broad Street to Yakubu Gowon Street,' the man said.

'Yes, Yakubu Gowon Street,' she said.

'You have a friend there?' he asked. That's better, Amaka thought. The silence was deafening.

'No, I don't have a friend there. I am going to submit a letter of application to the Ministry.'

'Do you have anybody there? Anybody you know, I mean?'

'I have a note from my brother-in-law to give to one Alhaji there.' She said the name of the Alhaji and the man smiled.

'I am the one.'

Amaka was so pleased she did not know what to say. Was

43

this a coincidence? This was too good to be true. Was this planned? Who planned it? Was she that lucky? She had never regarded herself as a lucky woman. If she had been lucky, her relationships with men would not have been so chaotic and unsatisfactory. Now she was in Lagos to start a new life. Perhaps things would begin to get better for her now. Everybody she had met so far had been good to her, her sister, her brother-in-law, Adaobi and her husband, and now this man.

'You know my brother-in-law then?' she asked.

'I know not only your brother-in-law but your sister Ayo as well. I saw you when you were leaving the house this morning. In fact, I saw you the day you arrived. Your sister is not sociable. I think she likes to keep to herself. She strikes me as a very intelligent girl, and I admire the way she takes care of her children. This morning I woke up at five thirty and I saw you leaving the house. I said to myself where is this woman going this early morning? I must find out. So I got ready for work and took the bus route and I saw you at the bus stop still waiting. Well, to cut a long story short, your brother-in-law and my family are great friends. We saved him during the civil war. When the soldiers came for him in Jos because he was an Ibo, I prevented them from taking him away. I told them that they would take the two of us to whoever their commander was, and they would all be court martialed. They were afraid, and left him alone. Very early the next morning, I sent him away to my village not far away. He was there in hiding for six months when I went and fetched him back. By then things had settled down. The soldiers were no longer as wild as they had been, and we have remained friends ever since.'

They were now near the Ministry. The Alhaji parked the car and opened the door for Amaka. In the office, he asked for the application, called someone to take the details of the application, and asked Amaka to go. She would hear from him later.

Amaka was surprised to receive a contract for the supply of toilet rolls worth ten thousand naira. She could not believe it. Toilet rolls worth that much, without her giving anybody any money? It was not so in Onitsha and Enugu. Before one saw the big boss, one first of all saw the messenger who would then tell the big boss that someone was waiting. If one did not 'see' the messenger, no way. Her files went missing each time she finished a job. When she learnt what was expected of her, her files no longer got lost.

Before the war, a government official rarely ever asked for a bribe. If you gave him a present when the job was accomplished satisfactorily and you were paid, he was grateful. Alas, it was no longer so. You had to give money first before you are even considered for a contract.

To register her company in Lagos, she had to go straight to the man who dealt with it. Of course, she was introduced, and in a matter of days, she got her company registered. It usually took people two or three years before a company was registered in Lagos. Lagos was good for her, Lagos was kind to her. She must, of course, be very careful. She was not going to be involved again with men. She had had enough. She had not come to Lagos to be a whore. She had come to look for her identity, to start all over again. Nobody was going to mess up her life any more.

With the help of her sister, she was able to raise money from the bank and supplied the ten thousand naira worth of toilet rolls to the Ministry. She made a gain of three thousand naira outright. She could not believe it. Three thousand naira of her own!

She looked for a flat and moved in. She went to see her friend Adaobi from time to time. She told her of her good fortune. Adaobi was glad for her, but Amaka could see a bit of envy. She was sensitive and noticed it. It was there for certain. And she decided that she was going to be careful in future. She was not going to take her into her confidence that

45

way. She was not going to let her know how much money she was making.

That night Adaobi told her husband. 'Dariing, we are wasting our time in the Ministry, you know, working ourselves to death and getting meagre salaries and thinking that we are doing marvellously well. Look at Amaka who came to Lagos the other day, making so much money in just supplying toilet rolls.'

'You want a company registered?' he asked.

'None of your jokes now.'

'I am not joking, Adaobi. I mean it. If you want to register a company, first resign your appointment in the civil service, and start hopping from one Ministry to another. It is either one thing or the other. You cannot do both. Perhaps when you go to these Ministries hunting for contracts, you might as well tell them that your husband was killed during the war, and that you were left with fifteen children to look after. Add also that your husband's elder brother wanted to marry you, but you escaped with your fifteen children and . . .'

'Stop!' Adaobi shouted and burst into tears.

'I am so terribly sorry, darling, please forgive me. Did I go too far? How can you be a contractor? I cannot bear to think of you as a contractor. Your friend envies you. You have me and you have our children, a good job and this house.'

'This house is not our own. The government owns it. One day the government could fire you and we would have nowhere to live. We have no house at home either.' She had wiped away her tears and was blowing her nose.

'Why now, Adaobi, why now?' Mike was confused. What was happening to his wife? Had Amaka come from Onitsha to unsettle their home? Adaobi had never behaved in this way before. She was such a contented wife and mother. Did she count the cost? The heartaches that Amaka had to go through before she was able to make that profit? Did they always make profit and no loss? What was Amaka going to

46

give to the Alhaji in return for the contract? And would Amaka continue to get that kind of contract?

He would speak to the Father. His wife was behaving strangely these days. So Mike found himself at the Father's sitting room in the evening. Just as he was about to sit down, Amaka drove in in a taxi. 'So Amaka knows the Father's house,' Mike said to himself.

The Father was surprised to see them and thought they were together. He served them soft drinks and when Mike got up to go, he followed him to the door. Mike somehow did not want to tell the Father why he had come. After all, he thought, how could a priest know the heartaches of a marriage when he was married to God? What advice was he going to give to him? Was he not over-reacting? Surely his Adaobi was not a bad wife. He had never complained about her to anyone, why start now?

'I was just passing, Father, when I thought I should say hello to you. We have not seen you lately. You are always welcome to our home. Adaobi would particularly like to see you during weekends or any time you are free.'

'I have been busy,' Fr. Mclaid said. 'There was lots of work to be done, and about a fortnight ago, I was asked to take over the job of Rev. Fr. Stephen who had gone home because his mother was ill and he had to be with her. She is seventy. And you know how attached he is to his mother.'

'That means you will be going to the mess quite often and conducting Mass for the soldiers in their barracks,' said Mike. And then he knew why Amaka was there. Mike turned to Amaka.

'Young lady, it is delightful to see you. We haven't seen you since that day at your friend's. Have you started going to church? Your friend spoke to me about you and your problems. I wonder whether there is anything I can do for you?'

Amaka had come to see the Rev. Fr. for an introduction.

47

As she said and believed, she was much luckier in Lagos. She was at her sister Ayo's house when a group of young women came in. They were all contractors. Nearly all of them had lost their husbands during the war, and all of them had moved to Lagos because there were some army jobs to be done.

Amaka did not know any of them and Ayo, knowing how competitive getting contract jobs was, did not introduce her sister to them. Ayo was a schemer. She did not even tell Amaka why she invited them. All she told her was to be attentive. Ayo entertained them lavishly while Amaka listened carefully.

'Some people are lucky, you know,' began one of the women.

'Who is lucky?' another asked.

'Madam Onyei. All she did was send for her eldest daughter who was in school and left her to the mercy of men. Now she does not know what to do with the numerous contracts she has. She gave me one the other day and I made two thousand naira outright. I even did not bother to do it myself. I gave it to someone who just handed me two thousand naira in a week. So I went home and celebrated.'

'Madam Onyei must be making a fortune. She has built herself a house in her home town. Brought her aged mother to Lagos after buying a house at Ikeja. She is in the money,' said another.

'And do you know what? Last year she went for "summer" and said she would take her mother for "summer" this year.'

'No,' said Ayo. 'She must have an interpreter. She can neither read nor write.'

'She took a clerk who had been with her and her husband for years,' said another.

'I am just waiting to buy a house in Surulere or Ikeja. When I have done that, I shall leave Lagos and go home. There is lots to do at home. And I don't want my children to be brought up here,' said another.

'All my children will be brought up here. They will speak Yoruba and Hausa and other languages of Nigeria. The country is changing at a terrific rate, and one would be lost if one did not speak at least two of the main languages,' said another. They agreed with her.

They were the new generation of women contractors. There were about ten of them. Six were widows and the other four had left their husbands to start life again. They were all involved in the 'attack trade' during the war. Madam Onyei was one of them as well. Her husband was killed in July 1966. He was an officer, and the friends of her husband managed to bring her down to Lagos. She refused to go home to the East. She said she was determined to die in Lagos with her children. She was quite an independent woman, and she feared the kind of welcome she would receive if she went home to be a widow when there was a threat of war. So in Lagos she remained. Her late husband's colleagues, when things settled down, helped her by giving her contracts. She struck a business deal with one army captain. Both made fortunes during the war. The deal was so well-known in army circles that the captain was quietly retired from the army.

So Madam Onyei went on making money. The joy of having grows by having. So she went on doing bigger deals. And, at one time, it was even said that she had organised the exportation of hemp to Europe. This was being whispered around but nobody was sure. The way she threw about her money made people start to gossip. She did not bother, but went on making money and spending it.

Another woman in the group was a widow as well. In the coup of January 1966, the coup plotters came to her bedroom, knocked at the door and her husband opened it. They took him away, and she heard a shot. Her ten year old son screamed. One of the coup plotters came to the child's

49

bedroom, took him out and shot him. They took the two bodies away.

Yet there was another who was engaged in the 'attack trade' during hostilities. She went to one of the war fronts to buy cigarettes, batteries and 'guff' with some other women 'attack traders'. While they were sleeping in a hut, some stragglers attacked them at night. She was brave, she had a toy gun that belonged to her son. She always travelled with it. She received training in the militia and was able to shoot and to kill. When the war was getting too dangerous, she left the militia and got on with the 'attack trade' which was equally dangerous.

When the straggler woke her up demanding all she had, which was tied onto her waist, she pointed her toy gun at him. He panicked and she escaped. But the other women in the group were unprepared. They robbed them and shot one who resisted. The incident haunted the woman for the rest of her life.

One of the women was in a refugee camp with her six children when the planes descended and she lost three of her children. Those women all had stories to tell. All they cared for was themselves and their children if they had any.

'You know someone told me that the handsome priest was now the army chaplain. The old one has gone.' All the women showed keen interest.

'It beats me that such a handsome man could be a priest when these beautiful girls go about quarrelling over one man.'

'Not all of them go into the priesthood with their eyes open, mind you. They all have one reason or other for their action. But what I hate is what that priest was saying in the papers the other day. I don't see why a paper run by the government should give him such publicity,' a woman said.

'I did not read it,' Ayo said.

'Oh, I read it,' Amaka said. This was the first time she had joined in the conversation.

'I agree with you,' Amaka went on. 'Why should he criticise something he has been a part of all his life? If he wanted to leave the priesthood after taking his vow, he should leave quietly. He was not obliged to fight his war on the pages of the newspaper.'

Amaka was asked to tell the story. She told it briefly. She was so biased. 'Whatever was his reason for leaving was his private affair,' she concluded.

'We were talking about the handsome priest who is now chaplain,' one of the youngest of the group said.

'My dear, we are too old for him. The schoolgirls who are our own daughters have taken over,' another said.

'No, I don't mean it in that sense,' the woman who gave the information initially said. 'What I mean is this: we can now go through him to the Brigade Commander for contracts. The one who has gone was unapproachable. And I understand that this one they call Mclaid is sympathetic. He will be able to help.'

Adaobi's name was mentioned as one of the women who could help reach the handsome priest. Nobody said she was going to try. They were in a party mood. But everything registered in Amaka's mind. So that was why she was in the priest's house that day. What audacity! Before then, she would have gone through her friend, but she did not want to. She was finding her feet in Lagos. In a short time, she would find money to pay back the dowry and be free.

Paying back the dowry had occupied her mind ever since she left her husband's house in disgrace. She had vowed that if God spared her life she would work and repay the dowry. She had told Adaobi this, but the latter did not understand.

'It doesn't matter at all, Amaka. Why does it bother you so much?' she asked.

'You do not understand, Adaobi. You have children, I haven't. If anything happened to your marriage now, and you left or your husband left you, you would be all right, because you have children. I am not so blessed. According to our custom, if I died tomorrow I would not be buried until my husband was informed. Obiora is still my husband whether he drove me away or not. So I will divorce him according to our custom, so when I die he will have no say. My property will go to my brothers or my uncles. He will have no claim whatsoever.'

'What if you made a will?' Adaobi asked.

'I don't really know. I don't know which custom precedes which, the native law and custom or marriage by ordinance. Things are not clear. But I would first perform the native law and custom before I go into the law courts for divorce. It is cheaper and less involved.'

Amaka got up when Father Mclaid entered the sitting room again after seeing Mike out. Briefly she told him why she had come to him, explaining her marriage and her childlessness. She found it so easy to talk to him.

This was only their second meeting. Why did she find it easy to speak to this man of God? Was it because she believed that her secret was safe with him? Surely she did not hold strong views about priests and their work. She was a Protestant and not a Roman Catholic, and she was almost indifferent to what they stood for and believed.

She believed in marriage of the clergy if she was asked her opinion. That was more human. If one could still marry and be in the service of God, able to maintain one's family and react favourably to the demands of modern society, then a priest or a pastor was truly a man of God and in the service of God.

She trusted Father Mclaid. Why, she did not know. When they first met, she had asked about his name. But she had not given a thought to the name and the owner of the name until the day of the party at her sister's house.

'And Father, please don't misunderstand my motive for

coming to Lagos. I regard Lagos as my second home. I am at peace in Lagos. I have not come to Lagos to be a prostitute. I have come to start again. I have not been abroad, but Lagos is the place for me. Its size intrigues me; its people, everything about Lagos seems to agree with me.

'I want to live a decent life in Lagos. When you are in Lagos, nobody knows you are there, because it is so big. Onitsha is small and it will not do for me. I wanted to get out of the place where I suffered most. I don't want to be reminded of my life with my husband. It is too painful. And all my brothers and sisters with the exception of my mother are in Lagos, Kaduna and Jos.

'So I have come to you. I did overhear women talk about your new position. Perhaps you would help me secure a permanent contract there. It would be much easier for me. Then I could be more relaxed and take care of myself. For I believe, Father, that I must have children. The gynaecologists have had their say, but I know that a child will come in God's own time.'

She had finished. The priest went into the kitchen and came out with another bottle of Fanta and some cakes and biscuits, and placed them on the table for his unexpected guest. He was at a loss as to what to say. This was the first time this kind of request had been directed to him. He did not know what the job he had to do entailed. He knew he would be seeing a lot of army officers, ministering to their souls and all that. How was he going to ask any favours from them?

Amaka did strike him though. The way he looked at her at the first meeting. Did she know and was cashing in? It was obvious to the priest. Amaka herself knew that she had made some impression on the man of God. She was not a child. She was going to exploit the situation. What drove her to see Father Mclaid was just the contract and nothing else. Now other things were working in her mind. She would play it cool. For the first time she was going to put into practice what her mother had been teaching her. She was not going to wait, she was going for the kill. A priest was also a man capable of manly feelings. Father Mclaid was a man, not a god. Perhaps Father Mclaid had never been tempted. She, Amaka, was going to tempt. That was the task that must be done.

Chapter 6

Mike went back to his wife feeling very bad indeed. He was right in what he thought. Amaka was having a bad influence on his wife, and it must stop. What was Amaka doing in the Father's house? If she wanted anything from the priest, was it not courteous, expected even, that she should come to them and not go directly to the priest's house? Amaka met the Father in their home. Amaka was up to something. Mike was not going to allow it.

But then he did not know how to approach his wife on the matter. He did not want to upset her. Surely their marriage had the usual problems, but they had stuck together for twenty years. That was a long time for two people to be married and have stayed together. Mike not only loved his wife but respected her. He respected her views and he never deliberately hurt her. He was good to her. Of course he occasionally strayed like all men, but the affairs did not last. For one thing he was too busy, so he did not find time to have extramarital activities. He wondered why men did it. And his conclusion was that the men who were involved in it were unhappy at home and wanted a place, a neutral ground for relaxation which they could not find at home.

So this strange behaviour of his wife surprised him. Adaobi did not like to be involved in business. She had always said that she did not have the nerve to do business. She always said that business was insecure. A government job was secure. She had her salary each month and she budgeted very well. She never complained of the house-keeping money her husband gave her. If it was not enough, her husband did not know. But like a good husband that Mike was, he from time to time bought his wife expensive presents, and always delighted in giving her a surprise. What was happening now to Adaobi?

'Adaobi!' Mike heard himself calling his wife.

'Yes, Mike.'

'We haven't heard from John lately.'

'John? Oh, he's fine. I received a letter from him two days ago.'

'What did he say of the boarding house?'

'Oh, he said he loved the food. The boys are friendly and . . .'

'Did he say he was missing home?'

'Oh, Mike, how can he say that?'

'I miss him.'

'So do I.'

There was an awkward silence. Adaobi was busy getting ready for work. Mike wanted to take it easy that morning, so he was relaxed. Adaobi knew that he was up to something, but did not know how to introduce the subject. She waited. She was still thinking of her friend, Amaka, and her good fortune. She wasn't sure what she wanted to do yet. Three thousand naira is a lot of money to get in just under two months. She could register a company and ask her husband's friends to help secure some business for her. She could then ask Amaka to take on the job and they would share the profit. No, she was not going to get directly involved with supply. Well, in that case, she thought there was no need to register a company. Amaka already had one. They could use that.

'Darling,' Adaobi heard her husband call. 'I saw Amaka at the Father's the other day.'

'How long ago?' Adaobi asked without interest, but the sharpness of the answer did not escape her husband.

'What's the matter, Adaobi?'

Adaobi feigned surprise. 'What have I done wrong?'

Mike there and then concluded that there was something really wrong.

'You said you saw Amaka?'

'Was it wrong to say I saw Amaka?'

'No, darling.'

'But when I said I saw her, you immediately became defensive,' Mike said.

'Defensive?'

'I said defensive. You were about to defend yourself against what I was about to say. Well, let me say it now, since we have got this far. I don't like your association with Amaka, and I want it to stop. I don't want any explanations. I don't want you to be hostile to her. If she comes here we shall welcome her, but you are not to visit her or to help her secure any contract, because I am not very sure what she is up to. I met her by accident at the Father's house. I don't like it. They say these Biafran women have a way of getting to men in high positions. Read the papers where women are crying that these girls from Biafra were snatching their husbands from them.'

'And just what are these wives doing when the girls are snatching their husbands, sitting back and allowing it to happen?' Adaobi said. And Mike was impressed.

'Are you going to put up a fight for me if a Biafran girl wants to snatch me from you, Adaobi?'

'A Biafran girl dare not in the first place. But that is neither here nor there. Those husbands who are snatched are those who want to be snatched,' said Adaobi. 'If you are unhappy at home, and discontented then you could be snatched. But if you are well taken care of like I am taking care of you, why should you be snatched?'

Mike was happy to hear this theory, but he knew that the world was not all that simple. There were terrible complications. He had had several affairs with girls before he finally married Adaobi, and he was surprised that she was a virgin. But then from what he had heard about other people, especially husbands, virgins did not make particularly good wives. But like a man his ego shot up high. My, he was the first o see between Adaobi's legs. No other man had had the privilege. He was flattered. And again Adaobi had proved a good wife. He was blessed.

That was all the more reason why he was worried about these new and strange developments. How would Adaobi take this order from him? Would she defy it? They had in the past reasoned things together and had come to conclusions without one imposing his or her will on the other.

Adaobi wanted to ignore the order and talk about the Biafran female's attitude. In Lagos they heard a lot about the girls who turned soldiers overnight and slept in trenches with fighting soldiers. They wondered how a fighting soldier could fight after sleeping with a girl in the trench. Could he have the stamina to run or to fight afterwards?

Overnight the girls in Biafra had been let loose. Their villages had been sacked, their relations killed, they had escaped with sisters or brothers and had fallen on the mercy of Biafran officers who were only too glad to have them as troop-comforters, and to avoid their brothers being conscripted into the army, had also taken on the boys as their batmen. It was therefore not surprising to see more batmen than fighting soldiers in Biafra.

One could not blame the girls. They had to survive. At the end of the war, they had to 'survive the peace'. That meant that they had to start all over again, away from it all. So Lagos was a fertile ground: no brother, no sister, no cousin to say to the girls, 'Enough is enough. Why are you prostituting yourself? Go home to your parents.' For one thing, there was no home to go to. The war took care of that. The war destroyed family life as the girls knew it.

Those in Lagos did not understand. Even Adaobi and

Mike did not understand. The experience of the war was personal to those who lived it. You had to live through it to understand, and to prevent it from happening again, if you could.

Then Adaobi heard Mike saying something to their little girl and just then the telephone rang. The little girl ran and picked it up. 'Who is speaking?' she said in her childish voice. Mike went and took it from her.

'You don't say that, young lady. I have told you that you should say your number first.

'Hello, 2525099.'

'Good morning. Can I speak to Adaobi please.'

'Please hold on.' He covered the mouthpiece with his hand and said to his wife, 'Your friend would like to speak to you. Do I tell her that you are in the toilet?'

'My friend? Which one?'

'Wonders will never cease. Didn't I say that that woman was up to something? Where could she be phoning from this early morning?' said Mike.

'Who is it?' Adaobi asked again and made an attempt to take the telephone from him.

'Your friend, Amaka, is on the telephone. Can I tell her that you are in the toilet?'

'You will do no such thing, Mike. I want to speak to her. Am I a child? I want to speak to Amaka please.' She emphasised the 'please'. She was angry. Mike surrendered the telephone and stormed out of the bedroom. But he soon returned.

'Amaka, how are you? Where are you calling from?' b
'Adaobi,' the voice answered. 'It's been a long time. How are you? I have been so busy. I called to let you know that I am now on the telephone and my number is 0011088. Please take it down.'

'Great,' Adaobi said. 'Amaka, that's wonderful. You mean you have a telephone installed in your flat in Surulere?

I can't believe it. How did you do it?'

'It's a long story, Adaobi. I'll tell you when we meet. I am travelling to Onitsha tomorrow and will be back before the weekend. I shall phone again when I get back. How are Mike and the children? I hope they are well.'

'Very well. See you when you get back.'

She hung up and looked at her husband. 'What is the fuss about, darling? Why are you against her? She has to live. I don't understand all these warnings about her. Do you want her to disappear from the face of the earth?'

'Is she going back to her husband?' was all Mike asked.

'Going back to Obiora indeed! How could she go back to him?'

'It is better for her reputation.'

'What reputation? She has no child, Mike. She was a good wife. Her problem with her husband was her childlessness, haven't you heard?'

'Will the people she is now associating with give her children?'

'Meaning that she is sleeping with all of them.'

'I didn't say that,' Mike said.

'You implied it and I will answer you. If they will give her children, she will sleep with all of them one after the other. She will not even care who the father is, once she is pregnant. She went through hell on account of this, and she would bend over backwards to have a child from any man, even a beggar from the street. She has come to the conclusion that apart from Obiora, another man, any man, could make her pregnant.'

'In spite of all the gynaecologists said?'

'They could be wrong. Miracles do happen even nowadays,' Adaobi said.

Mike went to work rather late that morning. Amaka was still on his mind. A telephone in Surulere a few months after she had hired a flat? A friend of his had told him that he

60

applied for a telephone four years ago accompanied with a five hundred naira bribe, but he did not get the telephone. He kept visiting the P & T but no telephone. After two years, he was written a letter telling him to apply again. He was indignant. What happened to the five hundred naira bribe he gave? The man he gave the money to had, they said, been transferred, and a new man had taken his place. He had come with a kind of religious zeal to right all the wrongs of his grabbing colleague. So he had designed a new form and a new system. Everybody was to be treated alike. There was not going to be any favouritism. No underhand business.

The man applied again, but was surprised to be visited by a man who purported to have been sent by the very man who had come to clean up the place. He demanded one thousand naira. The man gave it to him in raw cash. Why not? If he had a telephone, he could sit down in his house and office and do his business. It was costing him time and money to communicate with his business associates both in the country and outside the country.

He waited a year but nothing happened. And now, in the fourth year and having paid one thousand five hundred naira, he had no telephone. The man who had demanded the thousand naira was nowhere to be found. When he lodged his complaint to the P & T, he was told that there was no such man.

And here was Amaka from Onitsha the other day, having a telephone. How many people was she going to call in Lagos? What were her business connections to demand a telephone? Nigeria was a unique place indeed. Anything could happen, and culprits get away with it. But what could people like Mike do? They were civil servants who were trained by the colonial masters. They found it difficult to work with the new breed who did not know their right from their left.

Bribery and corruption was the order of the day. It used to

be ten percent Ministers. Now kick-backs amounted to thirty to forty percent. Wasn't it time for people like Mike to think seriously of retiring honourably? People like him were now being relegated to the background. Their opinions did not matter any more. In fact they were no longer given the privilege of airing their opinions. Perhaps his wife was right. He had no house at home. He did not even have a plot of land in Lagos. What was he going to do if he was suddenly uprooted from Lagos?

He began thinking kindly of his wife. When he reached his office, he phoned her. But he was told that she was not in the office, that she had not shown up that morning. The time was nine-fifteen. 'Please find out whether she is on a ward round,' Mike said in panic.

'Mr. Man, I have told you, madam never come o, abi you no hear the English wey I dey speak.'

Mike replaced the telephone. That was the language he hated to hear in government circles. What did they teach the children in schools these days? Why did everybody prefer to speak pidgin English or Yoruba in offices? Were they now going to abolish English in government offices?

He was irritable. At eleven o'clock he phoned again, and again he was told that his wife had not come to the office. 'How unintelligent of me,' he said, and phoned the house. Adaobi answered.

'Darling, you did not go to the office. I phoned there.'

'Wonders will never cease. Mike, when did you start phoning my office?'

'Today,' he replied.

'Love so amazing, so divine, demands my soul, my . . .' and she began to laugh.

'What's so funny, Adaobi? What has come over you these days? Do I have to start wooing you all over again after four children? And why should I not phone your office if I feel like doing so?'

Adaobi was calm. Her husband was being worked up. He was up to something, but she did not want to spill the beans just then. She had made up her mind, the day that Amaka told her about her profit. She had realised that they were living in a fool's paradise. Living in Ikoyi indeed. Nothing was theirs except their clothes, cooking utensils and their children's toys. They hadn't even finished paying for their cars. And they were in a military regime where anything could happen at any time. She had made contacts. Her first task was to buy a house. She had not saved much, but she could borrow money from her bankers. She was not all that high in the Ministry, and she was married, so the Ministry was not going to give her a loan to buy a house. She would use her contact in Lagos and do just that so that if anything happened, she would find a place for her family.

'Darling, I am all right. I didn't feel like working today, so I phoned the matron, and she said I could have a day off. Are you satisfied, darling?'

'I am, thank you. But you are not playing truant like the others?' he said. He was so dutiful.

'Yes, I am playing truant for the first time in years. There are nursing sisters like me who take off for London after reporting sick. The same sisters get promoted when there is a vacancy. And we, the dutiful ones, slave on and on and stay where we are year in and year out. Just come home, darling. I have a lot of ideas. We cannot continue in this way any longer. We have children to take care of. We are just not alone. We have an obligation to our children. At least we should give them a decent place to live in and a good education if nothing else.'

Mike returned home before three thirty, had lunch and went to sleep. That evening he did not go to the office as usual. He stayed at home and watched television with his family. His mind was working. He hated new ideas, no doubt because of his training, but he agreed with his wife that they must now begin to think about themselves. Contract work was ruled out. He was prepared to consider any other new ideas from his wife except that. And it was not difficult for Adaobi to convince him that they must do something for themselves. Nobody would believe that they had been that long in Lagos without a house of their own. Mike was to make contacts as well. Buying a house was cheaper and better. True they did apply for land in Lagos, but were not given it. Mike did not believe in 'follow up'. But you got nothing today from government if you did not follow up an application for a loan or contract or telephone – in fact everything.

Mike began to think kindly of Amaka now. If she was instrumental in bringing home to him his past follies, then may God bless her. Why should he think that Amaka was going to corrupt his wife? Mike said so to Adaobi, and she made no comment. She knew what she wanted and she was going to get it just like Amaka. Whatever method Amaka was using was peculiar to her and her alone. She had made a lot of contacts in Lagos which she had not exploited. She was going to exploit them now for the good of her family.

So when Amaka came back from Onitsha, Adaobi paid her a visit. Amaka had never looked better than she was looking that morning. She had gone to Onitsha to see her mother who was ill. Her other sisters were rather busy and since she was the only one without a family so to say, she had to go. Her mother was improving. She had wanted to bring her to Lagos, but she would hear none of it. She wasn't leaving Onitsha for Lagos. She would remain in Onitsha. She said she did not want to die in a strange land.

'You know my mother, once she has made up her mind about something, you cannot convince her otherwise. She was a doctor and she was asked to take it easy. you know she has a big stall in the market, selling cloths of different kinds. But the smuggling which is rampant in Nigeria today,

64

hinders her business. She is afraid to buy smuggled goods, and smuggled goods are what our people crave for these days.'

Adaobi was not all that interested in Amaka's trip to Onitsha. She wanted to find out how she was getting on and then make a business proposal.

The two friends were eating when Father Mclaid came in. 'Father, you are welcome,' Amaka said and asked him to sit down. Adaobi was at a loss what to say. So Father Mclaid visited Amaka at her home. The other day, her husband saw Amaka at Mclaid's house, and now, here he was in the flesh. The Father was a bit shy or so it seemed to Adaobi when he saw her. It was obvious to Adaobi, however, that that was not the first or second visit; that Father Mclaid was a frequent visitor to Amaka's flat.

'Sit down and eat with us, Father,' Amaka said. And Adaobi gazed at them both. Amaka had changed a good deal. That was not the Amaka she used to know. But years had separated them, years of frustration for Amaka and years of fulfilment for Adaobi. They were bound to live different lives. They were bound to have different conceptions of life and how it must be lived.

Yet Amaka was at her best. Adaobi was not sure whether her friend expected the Father or not. She brought out food and they ate. It was so delicious that Adaobi forgot that she was on a diet. Adaobi asked for the recipe. She always asked for the recipe when she ate something she liked in the homes of her friends. As a good housekeeper, she had different kinds of soups to suit different occasions, and so she endeared herself to her husband.

Amaka told her that the fish she used in cooking the soup was bought fresh that morning, that was the difference. Otherwise she used all the same ingredients as Adaobi.

'So you don't put your fish or meat in the fridge?' Adaobi asked.

'No. I am alone here with my maid, and the market is not far. So when I return from my site, the maid cooks something for me, and it is eaten up. But you have a large family and you go to work so it is not easy for you.'

Father Mclaid ate without talking much. He was an easy sort of person, who endeared himself to his parishioners. When he visited them in their homes, he ate with them, and if they visited him and he was at table, they too ate with him. Just as Adaobi was busy rushing all over the place when Amaka visited her home, so did Amaka rush around serving and being a good hostess. 'Men,' Adaobi thought. 'Why should this lovely and homely woman not have a family of her own? Why was this denied her?'

As they ate, there was a knock on the door, and Amaka ran to open it. It was the Alhaji who had helped her get that first contract. The Alhaji liked Amaka very much and had made advances. But Amaka again did not feel up to it. The Alhaji had helped her secure more contracts and had helped in the execution of them. But he had never asked Amaka what profit she made. Amaka had told him about the three thousand naira she made on the toilet roll deal, but all he said was, 'Thank God, it is all yours.'

He did not eat with them, but sat down and was served soft drinks, while the others ate. Amaka did not want to be involved with the Alhaji. He already had four wives. Not that she wanted a husband, no, she did not want a husband. She wanted a man in her life. All women should have men in their lives. The men could be husbands or lovers. The Alhaji did not appeal to her that way. She did not want him as a lover but she could not yet make a clean break with him. He was precious to her just then. She needed him more than he needed her.

She had slept with him, of course, and was not all that thrilled with the experience. There was nothing about it. She was left cold and unsatisfied afterwards. It was like she was with Obiora, because Amaka began to realise during the troubles with Obiora that she no longer wanted him. She no longer wanted to have sex with him. When they did have it, for her it was an act of duty rather than love or affection.

Occasionally the Alhaji visited her, but the visit of that day was the first for some time. Amaka was suspicious. Perhaps he had come to call it quits. Perhaps he was angry with her. The last time he came, she had told him that she was having her period. But the Alhaji was not to be fooled. He asked her whether her period came fortnightly.

However, whatever he had come to say, he would not say it because of the presence of Adaobi and the Rev. Father. He sipped his soft drink, and when the others had finished eating, they joined him in the sitting room, while Amaka's maid cleared the table.

The Father was the first to take his leave followed by the Alhaji, who was somewhat relaxed in the company and promised to call again. Adaobi had come all the way from Ikoyi. She was determined to sit it out with the other guests. When they had all left, both women went into the bedroom. Adaobi was surprised when she saw Amaka's bedroom. She was not going to talk about that then, so she told her at once why she had come.

'You talked of your site,' she said. 'What do you do there?'

'You saw the Alhaji,' Amaka began, ignoring the question. 'He helped me get the contracts. He refused money from me. He wants me. You are married and living with your husband. Technically, I am married. I spoke to my mother about divorcing my husband, and do you know what she asked me? She asked whether I was pregnant by another man who wanted my baby. Of course I said no. Then she said in that case, I should not rush things, I should wait a little longer. But I don't want to wait. Well, that was just by the way. You know Lagos. No man can do anything for a woman, even if the woman is the wife of a head of state, without asking her for her most precious possession – herself. I must confess to you, I have slept with the Alhaji. There is a lot to be called 'Cash Madam'. If you can secure a contract through your husband's friends, who you know will never ask for the impossible, I am at your service. I have a site where I store timber and blocks. The Alhaji helped me buy the site. I hope to build a flat on it, by the grace of God. When I do that, then I will go home and divorce my husband.'

To Adaobi, Amaka's story sounded like a fairy tale. In under a year, she had accomplished so much, and she and her husband had been in Lagos for years and they did not have a plot of land they called their own.

'You are right, Amaka,' Adaobi said. 'I thought of this. No, I wouldn't be able to execute the contracts. I would get the contracts. Thank you very much. But one thing you should do for me is this, please never mention this to Mike.'

'Of course not,' Amaka said.

'How much did you pay to have your telephone installed?' Adaobi asked.

'Well,' Amaka began. 'Well, all I did was to tell the Alhaji that I wanted a telephone, and in under a week, I had it installed. I don't even know how much it cost.'

'You have arrived. You are about to conquer Lagos,' Adaobi said and they laughed.

'Adaobi, I was wasting valuable time at Onitsha. I should have left my husband after the second year when no child came. Well, God's time is the best.'

Her friend agreed with her that God's time was the best. They stood talking on the street. Then Adaobi entered her car and drove away. A minute later, Father Mclaid drove in. Adaobi did not see him because she went off in the opposite direction.

Chapter 7

'Amaka, you should have warned me that you were going to have so many visitors. I was so embarrassed.'

They were in the bedroom now and the maid had finished for the day and gone home. Amaka did not like the idea of maids living in. She preferred to live alone. She was an alone sort of person. Crowds scared her. She was most happy staying with a gathering of friends and relations. That was why the 'Cash Madam Club' did not appeal to her when her sister Ayo asked her to join.

'I am sorry, Izu. Adaobi phoned last night and told me that she was coming. There was no way of informing you. Your instructions, remember, were that I must not under any circumstances phone you. As for the Alhaji, he dropped in as usual. I have told you about him. Sit down and I'll get you some fried fish and beer.'

Amaka soon came back with the fish and beer. 'Where did you park the car?' she asked.

'The usual place. The little boy is watching it. He earns two naira for doing that. He is a delightful boy and I am thinking of getting him into school. He reminds me of my boyhood. I haven't told you about myself, Amaka. I want to tell you tonight. You remember your question, when I was introduced to you as Rev. Fr. Mclaid?'

'I remember very well,' said Amaka. She had changed into her nightie and was lying on the bed. Father Mclaid went and lay beside her.

'But I want you now, Izu. You can tell me afterwards, please.'

He kissed her and began to caress her. Much later, as they lay entangled, Mclaid continued:

'As I was saying, that little boy reminds me of my boyhood. I come from a village in Awgu where twins are frowned upon, even now. My mother was the second wife of my father . . .'

'Your mother is dead?' Amaka asked.

'Just listen to my story, darling,' he said, caressing her lovingly and gently. 'Unfortunately for her, she gave birth to twins, both girls. The villagers got hold of the twins and killed them. She was broken-hearted. For a long time she was not pregnant. She resigned herself to fate. She felt she was going to have another set of twins if she became pregnant again. So she avoided my father.

'But my father loved her dearly. He took her in and spoke to her, demanding that she should see reason, that it was the tradition of the land that twins must be thrown away. He told her that he had no power to go against the law of the land.

'My mother was not comforted. Then one day a friend visited her and persuaded her to go to church with her. She went along. She liked the church, and she continued to go, until she got baptised in the Roman Catholic church at Awgu.

'In a short time, the sisters came along and established a maternity hospital in our village. My mother was one of the women who worked hard to see that it was established. Through an interpreter, she told the Sisters about the inhuman practices of the killing of twins. She herself persuaded mothers to have their babies in the maternity hospital.

'But it did seem that there was something in our village that encouraged the birth of twins. More than thirty percent of mothers who came to the hospital had twins. They were afraid and many abandoned their babies there. Some women took the male or female depending on which they had more need of at the material time. Other mothers who were a bit more enlightened, fed one and left one to die of hunger.

'It is unbelievable that this practice still goes on today. The most recent one I was told of was a teenage girl who, afraid that she would have twins, went to the bush when she was in labour and actually had twins. She abandoned the male and took the female to a maternity hospital in Enugu. Later she was accused of murder. But when she told her story, the good female magistrate was sympathetic, set her free and condemned the inhuman practice.

'The maternity hospital did a lot for mothers who gave birth to twins. When the villagers knew that a mother had twins, and that the Rev. Sisters were protecting her and her twins, they made life very difficult for the family. When my mother saw that the Sisters were saving twins, she became more relaxed and so became pregnant again. But she had made many enemies in her campaign against the custom, and the people lay in wait to pounce on her if she gave birth to the offensive twins.

'My mother told me that she prayed night and day that God should not give her twins. She solicited the prayers of the good Rev. Sisters. But something told her that she was going to have twins, and that the people would kill them. She had this premonition, and pray as she did, it worried ner. The Sisters told her it would be all right and that she did not need to fear. But she was afraid.

'The day came. The Rev. Sisters were there to deliver her. It was a difficult birth. She cried and cried. She was going to have twins, God let her not have twins, please God . . .

'She gave birth to twins, me and my sister. My sister died twenty-four hours later, and two days later, my mother died. I became the property of the Roman Catholic church. The Rev. Sisters brought me up and the Rev. Father Mclaid who was in charge of the parish gave me my name, Francis

71

Ignatius Mclaid and adopted me.

'None of my relatives came forward to claim me. I was taboo. I would bring them ill luck, so it was good riddance that the white missionary had adopted me. They were a strange lot, claiming what should be thrown away. I lived with the priest. I served Mass. I was going to be a priest like the good Father who brought me up, who gave me life. Nothing else appealed to me. I was alone in the world. The Father was quite old; if anything happened to him, I would have no roots, nothing at all.

'Then came the coup. I was in the Seminary then. It was a great shock. I was regarded in the Seminary as one of the Irish priests, so they spoke freely when I was around. They took the coup quite seriously and made plans. They prayed and hoped that the upheaval in the country would not turn into a shooting war. Father Mclaid, my adopted father, was seriously upset. For one thing, he had regarded himself as a Nigerian and had no wish to return home to Ireland. He prayed the hardest.

'The war started, and Nsukka evacuated. Father Mclaid had gone there to see what was going on, to have first hand information. He refused to leave when the civilians were being evacuated. He was still praying when the Nigerian troops captured him and sent him to Lagos. The Irish High Commissioner reprimanded him and sent him home to Ireland.

'In Ireland, he was like a fish out of water. He just could not settle down. He missed me and missed Biafra. As God would have it, he heard of the delegation from Biafra headed by a very prominent civil servant who retired some years before. He was prominent in the Roman Catholic Church as well, and had been knighted by the Pope. My father was pleased and he, together with some other Irish priests and nuns who were in Biafra were asked to meet them and help them clear the way to be received by the Irish government.

72

'I was in this delegation and it was a very happy reunion for us both. I don't know why I was chosen in fact. But I think the Bishop understood my plight and felt I should join my adopted father in his home. So I went as the delegation's secretary.

'It was impossible for us to meet anyone in the British government and in the Irish Republic. The governments had made up their minds that they were not going to interfere in the internal affairs of Nigeria. Whatever help that was coming from Britain, Ireland and elsewhere would be purely individual and non-governmental. Recognition of Biafra and nearly eighty-five percent of her population as adherents of the Roman Catholic Church notwithstanding.

'There was nothing our delegation could do other than appeal to these organisations on humanitarian grounds to send food and clothing to the suffering masses of Biafra. Father Mclaid was disappointed and heartbroken.

'When we returned home, it took us two whole weeks to see our Head of State to report on our mission. The civil servants would not make the appointment. That was my first encounter with the Biafran civil servants. Going abroad was so easy, within twenty-four hours of briefing by the Head of State, we were airborne. Now nobody was anxious to know the outcome of our mission.

'I was sorry for the elderly knight and the way he was treated, but could do nothing. But he was a patient man and he calmly waited. Eventually we saw the Head of State, and gave our report. Whether he was impressed or not, we did not know, but we accomplished one thing. Caritas and the World Council of the Church began to fly in food, medicine and clothing to Biafra.

'I was not happy at the way these commodities were distributed. Things got out of hand, and just when I was thinking of joining the fighting soldiers to fight for Biafra, a message from my father came through Caritas. I should go immediately to Dublin.

'In Dublin, my father lay dying in hospital. I just made it before he died. "My son," he said. "I am glad you have come to see me die. Soon this war will end and you will be back to the usual routine. Nigeria is different from Ireland in many ways. Many of us went into the order because there was nothing else to do. It is not so in your developing country. I should have given you a different kind of education if I had given a thought to it at the time. You would have belonged more to your people, now you are neither here nor there. You have your own conscience, you should work out your own salvation. If you in future feel that you have not done the right thing, that you are in the wrong vocation or profession, let your conscience guide you.

'"You owe me nothing. You will feel free to live your life the way you think fit. I absolve you of all guilt so that my memory does not haunt you. If I had had my way, if I could live my life all over again, I would have married and had a son like you and . . ." '

Amaka had been completely absorbed in Izu's story. It was now dark in the bedroom and she switched on the light. Izu was crying. She said nothing. She went to the toilet, got a clean towel and wiped his tears away. She caressed him, she touched him in forbidden places, and he was aroused. They made love again.

Amaka had succeeded in tempting him as she said she would. She was going to play her cards very well. It was the first time in her life that she had planned the total annihilation of a man, using all that her mother taught her, which she had sadly neglected because the spinster missionaries had taught otherwise.

When it was all over, Izu began again: 'When we buried my father, I stayed on in Dublin. I had no wish to return to Biafra. To keep my sanity, I worked hard, I tried to write but could not. I needed inner peace to do that. I had plenty of

74

time on my hands. It was peace I needed, but I could not find peace. What was left for me in the world was the Church, the priests and the nuns, and of course my God. There were no relations. Many of my village people had believed that I was dead. In fact it was said after the death of my mother that the twins died. So as far as my community was concerned, I was a non-person.

'The war raged on, and our Zik came to Europe and made that speech asking Biafrans to lay down their arms. I welcomed that appeal. There was at last someone who was appealing to our people to stop the war so that our men, women and children would stop dying. It was pathetic for me to hear a Biafran youth on being asked by a journalist why he was fighting, reply that he was fighting to stop Nigeria from killing them.

'Volunteers were needed to join Zik in his mission to Nigeria. I volunteered and joined the delegation. That was why I was in Nigeria before the war ended. I worked in army circles. I visited soldiers in the barracks and their trenches. I ministered to their bodies and their souls. I was liked by both the soldiers and their families. I stuck to my name, Mclaid.

'Nobody knew I was from Biafra except of course Zik and the administrator of the East Central State, because I worked closely with each of them at one time or another.

'No matter how hard I worked there was this restlessness, this inner tumult which persisted, and even when the war ended, the restlessness continued. I was not altogether innocent during my time in the Seminary, I must say. But it was difficult to pinpoint the problem.

'I made friends with families and when the war ended I came in closer contact with those who had been in Biafra. Your friend and her husband were good to me, and their house used to be a kind of sanctuary for me.

'Then it happened, the day I set eyes on you in Adaobi's home, and the pain and longing afterwards, and now this,

75

you and I here in the flesh having an affair, a priest having an affair with a married woman. Has it occured to you that you could be pregnant? You did tell me that day that though the gynaecologists had said that there was no possibility of your ever becoming pregnant that you felt you would one day have a child. I too believe in miracles.'

'Let's not talk of that now, Izu. You do not realise what you have done for me since we first met. Apart from the contracts and the money involved and all that, you have made me feel like a woman again. I had failed in practically all my relationships with men until I met you, and at the right time, so to say.

'I know what I am doing, but cannot help myself. I cannot admit this to anybody and I don't think you would either knowing our different positions. All I know right now is that I love to be with you as we are now, to love and cherish you. I live for today, only God can take care of tomorrow. If you feel guilty about us, at any time, please say so. If the relationship is involving you too much and you want a break, all you need to is to tell me plainly. But please don't, when you are tired of my company, begin to make excuses. This would hurt me more. I would still have pleasant memories of you if you tell me the truth.

'I am not young and have seen a lot and gone through a lot, so nothing really shocks me in that sense. I would bear a truth said truthfully than a lie, given deceitfully and . . .'

'No more. Get me more of that fish and beer. I must go home now.'

Amaka went off to get the fish and the beer. Izu got dressed quickly and looked at the time. It was past ten o'clock.

Amaka brought the food and drink and set the tray on a stool. She asked Izu where he was going.

'Oh, perhaps you can get dressed and see whether my car is there.'

76

Amaka dashed out frightened. If his car was stolen, then the truth would come out. People would begin to ask questions and then . . .

The car was there. The boy was still there. Other boys had joined him. But he did not give them the name of the owner of the car. 'If you stay with me, the owner will give us money when he comes,' said the boy.

Izu did not go just then. As he drank the beer, they talked business. Amaka was to go to the Brigade Headquarters in the morning where she would meet a Brigadier who would give her her next contract papers. All it entailed was twenty five percent of the profit.

Amaka was there in the morning, got the contract paper and nearly swooned. Half a million naira's worth of contract for building a wall round some barracks. She was a go-getter. She went to the barracks and was astonished to see that the job had been done. The wall had been erected. Perhaps she made a mistake. So she went back to the Brigadier, but he was not in, so she told someone who was there. He told her that she must be foolish to talk in that way. She should just send her bill for payment. Was she the only one who did not know what was going on? If she had met the Brigadier, he would just take the contract paper from her and give it to another person.

Amaka was paid half a million naira within four weeks. Twenty-five percent of it was hers. Amaka had finally arrived. She would now go to Onitsha, see her mother, pay back the dowry and come back to Lagos. Perhaps she would go abroad, tune herself up, see a gynaecologist and have a really good holiday.

No, she must first buy a house, so she could join the Cash Madam Club. Why not? So she hunted for a house, but saw none. But she could build a house on the site, as she had said she would. Now that it was difficult to buy one in Surulere, she would start building her own. Just a beautiful bungalow.

77

with three bedrooms would do, and plenty of grounds.

There was a friend of the Rev. Father who was selling his newly bought Peugeot 504. She got it for next to nothing. Izu helped her to get an architect who designed a bungalow for her and in under three months, her house was ready and she was set to go home to Onitsha.

When she got back to Lagos, she would see whether she could manage going abroad, but first things must be done first. If she could not, then she would go next year. But she must see Adaobi and Ayo before travelling home.

Ayo was as usual with her circle of friends. They were going to have a big do shortly and they were discussing what they would wear. As 'cash madams', they would be different. They had branches all over Nigeria, and since this outing was taking place in Lagos, the members outside would hire a plane. They were not going to allow the Nigerian Airways to mess up their outing. They had prepared for it and it must come off well.

Ayo knew the Nigerian Airways officials through her Permanent Secretary lover. She would go to him to make the necessary arrangements. It was quite easy. Ayo maintained a very good relationship with the father of her children. She still had her children living with her, because the legal wife could not bear to set eyes on either them or Ayo. Ayo kept her distance. What else did she want from her lover that she hadn't got?

The plane was arranged, and just as they were discussing what to wear, Amaka came in, chauffeur-driven.

'Yes, I was told you had bought a car. Congratulations,' one 'Cash Madam' said.

'It's secondhand,' Amaka said, playing down the whole thing.

'Second hand indeed. The car is brand new. Amaka, you are doing very well in Lagos. Congratulations,' another woman said.

'The trouble with my young sister is that she plays everything down. I tell her to talk big, that you are not recognised in Nigeria today if you are modest. If you make a profit of two thousand naira, say you made twenty thousand. People will respect you and give you more contracts. Is there ever a time people are asked to get together and declare how much they have in the bank? Never. There is no such time.

'So, Amaka, when you go home to Mama and they come to drink to the new car, don't tell them it is second hand. Of course, nobody talks of a second hand car these days, but a used car. You must let people know that you are doing well, and of course you are doing well.

'Now,' she turned to the ladies. 'My sister would like to join us in our club. She now lives in a house of her own.'

'Sis, please, not yet. I have not moved yet. I still have to buy the furniture and all that and . . .'

'What was I telling you? Modesty will kill you. Allow me to finish. Ladies, she came to Lagos a year ago and she has completed a bungalow and is about to move in, and she does not consider it a big achievement. Listen to me, you have done very well, my sister. There are women like you who were here during the war and did contract work, but are still living in one room, a rented room, in Yaba and Ebuta Metta and even Ajegunle.

'So just allow me. You have arrived and you are now eligible to join our club. The fee is only five hundred naira. We have our meetings every first Sunday in the month. We have our constitution. We are about to have an outing in Lagos next month which will be the talk of the town for a long time. So pay up.'

Amaka opened her bag and gave her a cheque for five hundred naira.

'Cross it,' her sister said, and she did so. 'This is an exclusive club and I am not the one to mess up accounts.'

'Great!' the women shouted and welcomed her to their

79

'Cash Madam Club'. They ate and drank champagne, and Amaka felt like one of them. Later she drove to Adaobi's place.

At Adaobi's home, Mike was gardening and Adaobi was in the bedroom with their little daughter. Mike stopped his work and welcomed Amaka with open arms. He was no longer jealous of her. His wife had won him over and made him start thinking of retirement rather than thinking all the time about his job.

'Yes, Adaobi said you had bought a car. Congratulations.'

'Thank you. A brand new one at eight thousand naira,' she lied. She was learning fast. Wasn't that what her sister had taught her? The car had cost her only about four thousand naira.

'We must celebrate. Adaobi, come down, your friend is here,' Mike called. Adaobi came down quickly and embraced Amaka. She had been able to do a contract for both of them and had given Adaobi two thousand naira. Adaobi had bought a piece of land at Ikeja, and was planning to start building without a word to her husband. Meanwhile, her husband had applied for a piece of land in Victoria Island and hoped for the best. He had also filled in the forms for buying a house at the Festac village.

Adaobi brought out a bottle of whisky and gave it to her husband, who opened it and poured some drinks. The driver opened the bonnet and boot of the car and drops of whisky were poured in from the bottle.

'We ask for God's blessings,' Mike said.
We ask God's mercy,
Amaka to your health
Goodness will follow your footsteps
In this great city of Lagos
Where fortunes are made
Where fortunes are unmade

80

Lagos that makes and
Lagos that unmakes.

Your sojourn in Lagos
Has been a blessing
To you and to your friends
May your cup never dry.
And this car,
These four wheels
Will take you, safely
Wherever you go.

No enemies will bar the way
When enemies are in front
May you be behind
When enemies are behind,
May you be in front.
You will go safely
And return safe.'

Then he turned to the driver and spoke sternly to him, 'How
long have you been a driver?'

'Five years,' the driver lied.

'Let me see your driving licence.' The driver brought out
his driving licence.

'But you told me you had driven for five years.'

'Yes, sir. I have driven for five years.'

'When did you get your licence?'

'Oh, last year, but I had driven for four years without a
licence.'

'Can you drive a car to Onitsha?'

'I can, sir. I have driven many times to Onitsha.'

Mike turned to Amaka. 'Watch him and never be soft with
him. Never allow him to use your car carelessly.'

They went inside to eat and to celebrate the purchase of
Amaka's Peugeot 504.

Chapter 8

Obiora sat with his mother, feeling very worried indeed.

'Why are you worried?' his mother asked him. 'Just tell me why you are so upset.'

'Why shouldn't I be upset? You have driven away Amaka and the mother of my boys. Are you now going to be my wife?'

'How dare you talk to your mother in that way? How dare you?' As she lifted her hand to strike him, he dodged but held her outstretched hand in mid-air.

'Now, listen to me, Mother, listen very carefully to me. I hear Amaka is coming home and I am going to see her. I am going to beg her to come back, and you are not going to interfere in any way, because if you do, I am going to kill you. It is not an empty threat. I am going to kill you.

'A man must have a home. Why don't you go back to your home and leave me alone? Why don't you go to Obiozo? He lives in Okigwe with his wife, why don't you go there? Why must you run my day-to-day life? Because of you I got the wretched woman who is no wife at all. She had the boys and when she moved in, you would not let her be, and she has taken the two boys away, and I can't trace her now. And here you are talking about that stupid girl you call your friend's daughter. Who do you think I am to have anything to do with that girl? She is young enough to be my own daughter if I had married early. So no more of your match-making. As soon as Amaka returns, I shall go and see her and her mother.'

'You will do no such thing. I tell you, Obiora, you will do

82

no such thing, not when I am still breathing. Do you hear? Obiora, you wretched son, talking to your mother like that. I am leaving your house. You will come to me, you will come pleading that I should forgive you for the way you treated me today. Here it is,' and she drew a line with her forefinger as was customary. 'You dare to bring the whore into this house and you see what I, your mother, would do to you. You will know that though I am a woman, I am also a warrior, and . . .'

She left her son's house and brooded for days. She heard that Amaka was at Onitsha and that she was preparing to refund the dowry and all that. She also heard that she had refused to see her son, Obiora, and she was particularly happy at this news.

'Just what is that miserable son of mine going to do with the whore in Lagos?' Was she going to have a child now that she was prostituting herself in Lagos? That was the thinking of people at home. Any woman who was unmarried and lived in Lagos was a common harlot. It did not matter whether she lived the life of a nun, she was a common harlot and nobody at home would marry her. She had been condemned by her own home community. The same community would go to her for financial help if she had made it, claiming that they were close relations.

And that was the experience of Amaka when she returned home to her mother. News of her fortune had travelled before her, and 'relatives' were eager to come and welcome her. But her mother was there to protect her against the numerous 'relatives'. Her mother directed her every movement.

'I want to know your plans,' she said to her. 'Obiora saw me before you returned. I don't know who told him you were coming home, but he knew. So he came to see me, his second visit to me since you left him. He talked about reconciliation, blamed himself for his thoughtlessness and all those stupid things men say to us because they think we are stupid. I listened to him until he finished. Then I told him to bring his mother with him, before you came, so that we could clear up the grounds for reconciliation.

'I never saw him again nor his mother. Later I heard he spoke to my sister and son-in-law, but nothing came of it.'

'What happened to the sons?' Amaka asked.

'The mother of the sons could not stay with Obiora's mother so she left with the boys.'

'But I heard the children are not really his.'

'No. They are his all right. I saw them on one or two occasions. Our people lie a lot. She left because Obiora's mother is impossible to live with. What is your plan? You have not told me.'

'I have come to return the dowry to Obiora. Later I shall start divorce proceedings in the court. I understand it takes quite some time. You see, Mother, I want to be free, absolutely free.'

'Apart from your contracts and all that, are you happy in Lagos?' her mother asked. The people, contrary to Amaka's mother's ideas, believed that once a man or a woman had money, he was happy. He could buy happiness and contentment.

Amaka hesitated before she answered. There was a lot she was now learning from her mother. Her mother had changed quite a bit. She was no longer harsh, and there was some respect in her voice when she spoke to Amaka now. What did this changed attitude mean? Was it because of her status? Was it because she now had money and could speak from a position of strength? Even her mother respected money. But who did not? Her new wealth had changed her life somewhat. She knew how important it was for her to travel to Onitsha that day at the airport, so she bribed her way through. She had to give thirty naira to an official for a boarding pass. That was a thing she could never have done before she went to Lagos, and made her fortune.

There was that air of importance now, and she could feel it, and what's more, she loved it. Money was meant to be spent. So one should spend it when one had it.

'I am reasonably happy, Mother. I work hard and I have friends. Ayo is of course there, and she has introduced me to her circle of friends. So I am quite contented.'

'You are not living with a man?'

'No, Mother. Oh, Mother, what questions you ask!'

'I am your mother, you know.'

'Mother, but how can we talk about such things?'

'Why not? We are women you know. I am your mother. I know how you feel.'

'Mother, I am through with men. Let's talk about other things.'

'But I thought you were sending back the dowry because there was someone else and . . .'

'No, Mother. I have said goodbye to husbands.'

'That's better. Goodbye to husbands, not goodbye to men. They are two different things.'

Amaka laughed aloud. 'Mother, you are great. Of course you are right, Mother, you are always right. If I had listened to you in my youthful days, I would have had children without a husband, like Ayo. Mother, Ayo and I get on very well. She is a sweet sister. Of all my sisters she is the one I am really attached to.'

'Yes, Ayo is good. But you must love all your sisters equally. You must stay together. You cannot be alone in this world. You need people, relations, blood relations to go through life.

'Now, about Obiora. You are sure you don't want him any more?'

'I am positive.'

'He must be told then. Leave it to me.'

In the evening, Amaka's mother went to see the eldest man

85

in Obiora's village and told him: 'We shall come as is customary. If you don't accept the dowry, we shall leave it at your shrine.'

There was nothing Obiora could do, especially as his mother did not support him. If his mother were behind him she would have raised hell.

'Now that we have taken care of that, my daughter, you should invite your age-grade. They are entitled to share in your fortunes.'

So they were invited and they made merry and asked God to give Amaka tenfold of what she had spent in entertaining them. Just before they dispersed, one of them came alone and said, 'I understand you want to divorce your husband. Is that true?'

'Yes, but how did you know?'

'Well, I am a lawyer and I offer my services. My speciality is divorce cases.' Amaka laughed out loud. 'Yes, we too must eat. Marriages are made and unmade.'

They laughed. And this incident reminded Amaka of one of her friends who told her how she went to an office where marriages were dissolved instead of the proper registry. The man stared at her and begged her to be careful of the man she was about to marry. And it was prophetic because the man she was about to marry turned out to be a ne'er-do-well, who was deceitful.

Before she went back to Lagos, Amaka's mother told her of a native doctor, a woman who was very good at making women pregnant. She did not lose anything by going to this woman, her mother told her. She had heard of barren women who were treated by this woman and they became pregnant. Would Amaka like to visit her?

Amaka said she would and, that evening, they drove to the woman's hut in a very remote part of Onitsha. Amaka wondered how anybody could live in that place and not be sick. The hut was so low that, though she was not a tall

86

woman by any standard, she had to stoop to go in.

The hut was a mud one with a thatched roof. The floor was bare but for a small stool used in pounding fufu. The bed was a bamboo one with all sorts of rags on it.

The woman was at the back of the hut. She asked them to sit down and told them she would be with them shortly. She was busy with a client and Amaka and her mother had come too early.

When she came out, Amaka was surprised that she was a young woman, about her own age. Her appearance was clean and tidy. She welcomed them profusely, obviously having heard of Amaka and her mother.

She looked at Amaka and smiled a knowing smile.

'I am glad you have left your husband,' she began. 'He would not have given you a child. It is not your fault, it is not his fault either. You are just not compatible, that's all. Your case is a difficult one, nevertheless, because you should have had children before this new wealth of yours. Again it is not your fault . . .'

'Whose fault is it then?' Amaka's mother asked impatiently. 'If I had known you were going to talk in this way, I would not have brought my daughter. I have heard of your reputation, and I thought you would help, so no nonsense please. Will she have a child or not? Who is responsible for her barrenness these long years? We are not barren in my own family, neither are there barren women in her own family. There must be a cause for this. What is it?'

'Mother, don't be impatient with me. I know my job well, and no doubt you know yours. I say what is revealed to me by the gods. I don't say what my clients want to hear. If you are not satisfied with my approach, here is your consultation fee. You can leave.'

'Let's go, Amaka. What nonsense. Let's leave this dirty place. I didn't come here to be insulted.'

'Mother, wait. Why are you not patient? I used to think

that the blood of the young burns in their veins and they act rashly. I am discovering that the young are even more tolerant than the old. Go on, I am all ears. I want to hear what you want to say. Yes, the fault is not mine, it is not my husband's either. What can be done? Is there a remedy?'

But the harm had already been done. The woman could not go on. She had been disturbed. She could no longer communicate with her gods. She could no longer see anything, and she said so.

'You can come again if you want to,' she said to Amaka, greatly offended. 'There is nothing more I can do today.'

'Stupid ass,' Amaka's mother said, storming out. Amaka could not resist smiling as her mother spoke in English. That was the only abusive remark her mother could say in the language.

'Let's go home, my daughter. God's time is the best. You will have a child, in God's name you will have a child. Do not worry. She knows nothing. What did she mean by new wealth? That was why I was angry. Hadn't she heard of me and your late father and all your ancestors? Why should she talk of new wealth as if wealth was not in my family and yours?'

'But, Mother, you should have listened to her.'

'Listen to her insult us? And what do you call that? Good breeding? The trouble with you children who went to school is over-tolerance. You tolerate nonsense. You suffer fools too gladly. You get hurt and you hide your hurt. I don't understand you at all. I was witness to a delightful drama the other day.'

They got into the car and drove home. Amaka's mother continued:

'I saw a woman hold her husband's trousers in the street as he was entering his car to go to work. The woman kept shouting: "You can't go to work today without giving me soup money. What do you want me to do? Starve with my

88

children while you to go to work? You must give me food money today, this very day." Passersby collected as usual in Onitsha streets. The man was embarrassed. He fought, but the woman was resolute. "Soup money, no soup money, no work." That woman did not go to school. If she had, do you think she would have had the face to fight on the street? Of course not,' she went on, 'but she got what she wanted. Her husband was so ashamed that he wished the ground would open up and swallow him. That's it. That's what our men want these days. That's by the way. The woman is no use. She was not going to be effective either. I saw her, sized her up and spoke to her, so don't worry.'

That day the native doctor woman was visited by Obiora's mother. If Amaka and her mother had remained, both parties would have met face to face. The drama would have been too complicated to be described.

Obiora's mother said, 'I have to see you. I have a problem. It concerns my son who wants to marry a harlot from Lagos. Well, not exactly. She was my son's wife, and she nearly killed him, then ran to Lagos. And now my son wants her back. Can you believe it? Wants a harlot back while there are so many girls here wanting husbands. You must prevent this foolishness of my son's. He must not go to Lagos. He is threatening to follow her there. You must prevent this. That's why I'm here. I want my son here, here with me.'

'I have had enough for one day,' the woman dibia said. 'Now wait and let me hear you properly. You have come on account of your son and this woman that he wants to follow to Lagos, am I right?'

'You must be daft. Of course, yes.'

'You do not mean that this woman lives in Lagos and your son is here and . . .'

'Oh, my God. Did I have water in my mouth when I was speaking?'

'The woman you are talking about just left here with her mother.

'Say that again.'

'Did I have water in my mouth when I spoke?'

'No. Why were they here? To kill my son? Did they ask you to kill my Obiora? How much did you take from them and I will give you the amount a hundredfold. Talk, talk . . .'

'Hold it, hold it. I never reveal anything about my clients. Not even when they insult me. Say why you are here. Just tell me your business.'

'You dibias are all the same. You are all deceitful. Why did you whet my appetite? Did I see your clients? Did I ask you questions about who came and went? Weren't you the one who started it all, you miserable, poverty-stricken woman?'

'Who is insulting my wife? Who is the son-of-a-bitch insulting my wife?' The husband of the dibia had come in and heard it all.

'You'd better ask your wife to behave or else I'll insult her the more,' retorted Obiora's mother. 'I am not one of those she can trifle with. Oh, you are the one, I know you. Of course, I know you. Is that your wife, the dibia? But I saw her the other Sunday receiving communion. Is she a dibia?'

'And what are you doing here if you are a Christian and a communicant? You are not supposed to come to my wife. However, if you do not know, let me tell you, my wife is a good midwife. She received her gift directly from God above. She does what God asks her to do. She helps women to get pregnant, and that should not be against the teaching of the Church. Why are you here anyway? You have passed childbearing age. What do you want from my wife?'

'Our gods tear you to bits! Who has passed childbearing age? Your wife?'

'Please leave her, my father,' the dibia pleaded with her husband. 'It must be my fault. I have not had a good day today. I must do something to appease the gods. I have never been insulted in this way before. And this year is the tenth

90

year I have been in this profession. I have made many women pregnant. I have never done any harm to anybody. But this woman, and the one before her, came here to annoy me. Perhaps the gods are angry with me.

'Woman, go away. My business is to make women pregnant, not to prevent husbands from joining their wives. Your son has lost his wife forever, nothing binds them any more. So go away. Your son did not suit his wife, so she too has gone away, never to come back to your son. Now go away and leave me in peace. I can say no more. I have said what I have been asked to say, no more. Go, I have heard enough for one day.' She turned to her husband and said:

'Our father, welcome.'

'You have not finished with me yet,' Obiora's mother said.

'The devil himself has visited us today. Woman, what else do you want from my wife?'

'What is the fee? I pay my fees.'

'It is free,' the dibia said.

'Never. Nothing is free in our country today.'

'All right. Give her a head of tobacco.'

'Here is five naira for a head of tobacco.' And she left without saying another word.

When she got home, Obiora was waiting for her. She embraced him.

'That's my son. That's my second son, my pearl, my real son.'

'Where have you been?'

'To the market. I have had a good time in the market today. Sit down and eat with me. You look tired. What have you been doing to yourself?'

'I am fine, Mother.'

'You are worried. What is the matter?'

'Nothing.'

'There must be something.'

'Amaka is about to go back to Lagos and I heard she has

got a lawyer to start divorce proceedings. I don't want that, Mother. I hear she is very wealthy now. She has built a house in Lagos, she owns a car and she moves in very high circles in Lagos. She could be very useful to me. I want her, Mother. I am miserable without her.'

Obiora's mother allowed the words to sink in properly. She asked her son to go home and come again the next day. She did not sleep. She hadn't heard of Amaka's wealth until now. If she had heard, it had not sunk in until now. She had returned her dowry all right, but she could take it back. She knew how. The old men at home were poor. She knew how to deal with them.

In the morning she found out that Amaka had three more days in Onitsha before she went back to Lagos. She did not understand the court proceedings, but that would wait. Once she dealt with the dowry all would be well. She went to the head of the family. After the usual greetings, kola was brought and she put one naira on the plate for breaking the kola. The old man grabbed it as if he had never seen one naira before.

'I have come about my son's wife,' she began.

'Which one?' the old man asked.

'How many sons have I?' she asked evasively.

'I mean which of your son's wives?'

'I didn't know he had any other than the daughter of Okollo,' she lied.

'The whore who now lives in Lagos.'

'Just mind your tongue, old man. How dare you call my son's wife a whore?'

'I must be getting very old. What is today?'

'Afor.'

'And you are . . .?'

'Obiora's mother.'

'And this is my house.'

'Yes, I am in your house, and I have come to tell you to

92

return the dowry which Obiora's wife's people brought back some weeks ago.'

'To me?'

'Yes, to you. Obiora has made up with his wife, and they are both going to Lagos to live.'

'But, Obiora's mother, Amaka's mother said she would come but she has not come yet. I have not seen her. I should not accept the dowry just like that. It is not done. You seem to forget our customs. All my brothers come and I tell them and we decide. You know I never impose my will on my brothers.'

'God bless you. Here is another naira and thank you very much.'

In no time she was at Amaka's mother's house and fortunately found that Amaka was not in, but her mother was. Amaka had gone to look at a piece of land she wanted to buy in Onitsha, and her mother did not feel well enough to go to the market.

'Come in, come in. Obiora's mother, you are welcome to my house. Please sit down and make yourself comfortable. Welcome, welcome. I have just eaten. Shall the cook prepare something for you? I bought very good fresh fish. I can prepare it while you wait. Oh, welcome. What can I use to make kola? You are in my house, and I am greatly honoured. And the cook is not even here. Sit down, oh, you are seated. Let's see the fridge. There is nothing in it.'

They were all lies. The fridge was filled with all brands of soft drink and beer and stout. She did not want her guest to have anything.

Obiora's mother was, of course, not so easily fooled. They were both adepts at the game. Both knew what they wanted.

'Don't worry, Amaka's mother, or shall I say, my mother. Don't worry. I am on a course of injections and not allowed to eat kola or drink anything. I was just passing and thought I should pay you a visit and greet my daughter whom I heard

93

has returned from Lagos. I do wish these children could give me the eyes they used in seeing Lagos. I hear it is a most beautiful place, full of cars and bicycles and people, that it is easy to go to Lagos but difficult to return. My daughter has returned, so that saying has been proved wrong – well, for Amaka for course.'

'Lagos is a marvellous place, Obiora's mother. You must find time and go there. I never knew there was a place like that until I went there. My, why were our children dying during the war when there was a place such as Lagos?' Amaka's mother was pleased. At least, she had a clear edge on her enemy, the woman who wanted to destroy her daughter. She was under her roof. She didn't send for her, she came of her own accord, so whatever she got she deserved.

'And you need to go to Kano. My son, Chukwuma, is there with his white wife. They live in the area reserved for whites alone. And when I return from there I feel and look ten years younger. Then my son took me to a lake away from Kano. I could not believe my eyes. A lake in the midst of the desert, a lake as big, if not bigger than Oguta lake. Just in the middle of nowhere. I was amazed. I asked my son how they brought the lake to that place. And my son told me it was man-made. Man-made, can you believe that, that a man could make a lake and make fishes there as well? Obiora's mother, you must see Lagos and Kano and other places. This Onitsha has a way of making one old and sad and even ignorant.'

Obiora's mother knew she had asked for it. She began to blame herself but she soon recovered. None of the women had anything like regret in their vocabularly of words. What they did, and said at any time or place was absolutely right and must not be argued or even discussed.

'I am thinking of going to Lagos,' Obiora's mother began. 'So I thought Amaka could give me a lift in her car,' she lied.

'Of course, why not? She will certainly give you a lift in her brand new car. We poured libations the other day to celebrate the purchase of my daughter's car. I sent for you, but was told that you went to the funeral of a close relative. Oh, Amaka will soon come back. Wait for her. Actually, you would have the whole car to yourself after Benin, because my daughter will take the plane from Benin while you and the driver come by road.'

Amaka's mother had an edge over her. And she enjoyed it. 'Sure you won't drink anything? Not even a glass of water from the fridge? There is nothing like a glass of chilled water on a hot Onitsha afternoon.'

'You didn't go to the market today?' Obiora's mother asked.

'Market? Amaka came home and I am busy taking care of her, helping her entertain her friends and age-grade. I'll start again when she returns to Lagos. Oh, that's the sound of Amaka's car. She is back. You are lucky.

'Amaka, your mother-in-law is here. Can your dribver give her a lift to Lagos?'

It was too much for Amaka. She wanted to sit down first. She did not quite understand her mother. A lift to Lagos? Then she saw Obiora's mother and embraced her. 'Mother, it's been an age. Welcome. Nice of you to call. What is this that mother is telling me about Lagos? Are you going to Lagos?'

Obiora's mother nodded.

'I'll certainly take you. I leave next week on Monday, after service. But before then, I shall see you. And how are Obiora and the new wife or old wife and the sons?'

'They are fine. You look so well, my daughter. Lagos is kind to you.'

'She refused my kola and all I offered,' Amaka's mother said.

'Mother, did you? Never mind, in Lagos we shall have a lot

95

to eat,' Amaka said, and then Obiora's mother left.

Before six in the morning, Amaka and her driver were heading for Benin for Amaka to catch the first flight to Lagos.

Chapter 9

'There must be something wrong with me,' said Amaka to no one in particular. 'I have never felt like this before.'

It was nine o'clock in the morning and though she had so much to do, she was unable to get out of bed. The maid had arrived and was surprised to see her mistress in the house. Amaka was usually an early riser: by six in the morning she was already at her site directing the day's work and before nine she was in the Ministries either submitting the bills for jobs already done or waiting for another job order.

The maid was really a nanny whom Amaka called Auntie. She was a very dignified woman, but poor. She had had her share of good fortune in her earlier days, having lived with a sailor and had two lovely children by him. Quite contrary to the habit of white sailors in the West African coast at the time, Mr. W.C. Simon settled in Apapa, Lagos with his woman and kids. But then the Second World War came, and Mr. Simon was sent home to Germany. The order came so suddenly and unexpectedly that he did not make any plans for his family. He was an enemy of Great Britain, Hitler had declared war, and he, a German, had to quit the British colony.

Nanny was left to take care of the kids, a job she did admirably, for she had the means. Her sailor had left everything for her and the kids. But she was a poor businesswoman and very young. If she had had a good person to run the business that her sailor left for her, she would have done very well indeed. But she had two little ones to take care of, and had little or no experience at all in business. She must have been only seventeen years of age when she met the sailor.

She hoped and hoped that the war would end and her man would come home. At last the war ended in 1945, and a year later Mr. Simon sent messages, but nobody could trace his woman and children. She had changed location. She had gone home to Warri with her children.

Mr. Simon was disillusioned. He married a German girl, but always remembered his kids in Nigeria and their mother. Just out of the blue, Mr. Simon had occasion to visit Nigeria about 1955 and found his way to Warri. A few questions took him to the home of his Nigerian woman and the children. But a long time had passed. There was no question of taking the mother of his children with him. He had married. There was no marriage as such between him and the mother of his children. He was in a position of influence. He joined a company that came to establish business in Nigeria. Quick arrangements were concluded and the children went home with their father leaving a vague promise of their mother joining them later.

So Nanny saw herself in the employment of Amaka who treated her as an auntie. She knocked at the door and it took a long time before Amaka crawled out from bed to open it.

'My daughter.' (She always called Amaka her daughter because of the way she treated her.) 'Did you have a late night? I have never known you to have a late night since I have lived with you. What is the matter?'

'I am weak, just weak, Auntie.'

'Can I get you anything to drink?'

Amaka shook her head vehemently. She wanted nothing at all. 'I think I should stay in bed today and have a good rest. I need rest. Auntie, please pray for me, pray that I don't fall ill.'

'You will not fall ill, my daughter. You are a strong woman.'

Amaka smiled in spite of herself. 'Auntie, don't the strong fall ill?'

'They do, my daughter, but not you. You will not fall ill. Can I ask you one question?'

'Of course.'

'When was your last period?'

'When was my last period?' Amaka repeated to herself. Then she went to the bed and sat down and asked her nanny to sit beside her. She used to keep a record when she was married to Obiora. She did this so religiously that when nothing happened to her, that is when she did not become pregnant, she was very upset and hurt. That was, of course, before the gynaecologists had discovered her blocked tubes.

Since she came to Lagos, she had not bothered about periods any more. What did it matter to her? She did not lose much anyway so that any time it came, it was welcome, but when it did not come, she did not notice.

But she did remember that she had menstruated at Onitsha when she visited her mother, and that was some months ago. How long ago?

'Auntie,' she said aloud. 'When did I return from Onitsha?'

'I came to live with you three months before you went to Onitsha and it is two months since you came back,' she said. She was good at keeping records in her head. Had she not counted the days until her sailor would return to see her and the children?

'I have not had a period since that last one in Onitsha. So . . .'

'So you are to take it easy and stay in bed and not excite yourself too much, and . . .'

'Oh, Auntie, but . . .'

'My advice is this, see no one until you have missed it for the third time. Then go and have a urine test. If you are pregnant, it will show in your urine. God works in very mysterious ways, my daughter.'

'I have given up hope, Auntie.'

'Don't think about it, my daughter. The secret is between the two of us and, of course, your man. So . . .'

'My man, my man?' Then it dawned on her. Father Mclaid was the father if she was indeed pregnant. She had had nothing to do with any other man for the past four months. The Alhaji had dropped out of her life when he discovered that Amaka was merely tolerating him. He did not want her temporarily, he wanted her for ever. He wanted to own her, to keep her. Which was more tolerable, to be a wife or to be a mistress? She could not say. She did not know which was the lesser evil. She neither wanted to be a wife any more, nor be a mistress, or even a kept woman. She wanted a man, just a man and she wanted to be independent of this man, pure and simple.

In that case, she was perfectly all right. Rev. Fr. Mclaid would never, never want marriage nor would he claim her child. Oh why, why was she counting her chickens before they hatched? And could it be possible that she of all women should be pregnant now?

She had the urge to phone Adaobi, but restrained herself. What was she going to say to her?

'Can I have some coffee, Auntie?' she asked the nanny, who was now cleaning the bathroom.

'My daughter, I cannot give you coffee. You must not drink anything hot now. If you are thirsty, you can drink cold water.'

Amaka was in no mood to drink cold water and she was not hungry.

'You don't want cold water? Perhaps I can make breakfast for you.'

So Nanny made some breakfast. When Amaka finished eating she went straight to bed again. When she woke up it was almost noon.

The realities came back to her. What was she going to say

to the man of God if it was true? She pushed the thought out of her mind, had a bath and went to Ayo's house. Ayo was there as usual. She complimented her on her good looks and told her that the Cash Madam Club was scheduled to go to Ibadan the week after to launch the club. Amaka said she would be there.

Amaka was afraid to confide in her sister. 'Not now, not now,' she said to herself. 'When it is established.' But she was sure. That sort of thing had never happened to her before. She must do as her nanny told her. So when she had passed the third month, she took a sample of her urine, labelled it with a fake name and gave it into a diagnostic laboratory near her home. The test was positive, and so she was pregnant.

She was going to be grown up and sensible about it. Nanny came and lived in now so that she would have someone by her side at all times. Then she remembered, there was a time she was told by someone that she was going to be pregnant and the person responsible was going to be a special person. She was offended by that prophesy many years ago. So that man or woman was right after all.

She registered at a clinic that was close by so that she did not have to travel far. Then she gave up contract jobs for the meantime, and actually dropped everything, concentrating on her pregnancy and thinking of the best way to break the news to Izu, her lover.

Father Mclaid had been around at this period but he suspected nothing and Amaka told him nothing either. Amaka refused all his advances and he was getting upset about it. It worried him, but he said nothing to her. He had loved her with a great passion which was mature and considerate. Like Amaka, Father Mclaid knew that he was playing with fire. He had asked during the early stages of their relationship what would happen if Amaka got pregnant but she told him that she was not going to get pregnant. She did not elaborate and he did not press the issue. Amaka was quite impressed by that question, because it did show that Izu knew what he was doing, that he was responsible. She wanted just one thing from him at the time, a base where she would gain contract jobs, make money and live an independent life. Her association with the priest was not motivated by any feeling of affection, least of all love, at the beginning. Even now, she did not know what she felt for him. She did not miss him when he was away. He had warned that she must not phone him at home, and this arrangement suited her very well.

Izu was playing with fire, he knew it. But the last thing he suspected was that one day Amaka would get pregnant, and he would be the father of the offspring. He did not make any demands on her though he loved her. When he came to see her, and she was not in, he did not ask questions. Why should he?

But, as a man of God, sworn to celibacy, what did he think he was doing? Cheating God and cheating his flock? He knew he was committing a mortal sin, but he did nothing about it. At one time, he had thought of going to the Bishop to confess all, but he did not have the courage. Yet he did his job well. He was respected by both his congregation and his colleagues. Sometimes he felt so guilty that he was afraid to associate with his colleagues lest they know his thoughts. Sometimes he imagined that they knew and would one day expose him and he would leave the priesthood in disgrace.

For in fact what other profession was he good at except ministering to God? Other priests were professionals. There were doctors, teachers, even architects. He had not learnt a trade. He was good at preaching and he could convert the devil himself if he put his mind to it. He was not equipped at all to live a civilian life. When he came to Amaka he came in mufti, he sneaked in and out. Even the boy who watched his car in those days did not know that he was a priest. He was a careful man and he covered his path very well. But he knew that sooner or later something would happen. There was always a beginning, a middle and an end to everything, especially with an affair like the one he was having with Amaka.

What would be the outcome of it all? He did not want to pursue the thought any further. So he pushed it to the back of his mind as Amaka had done. But then the thought nagged him night and day. Then he began to remember Amaka's behaviour of late. Why did she avoid him? Why did she not want to have sex with him any more? Was something happening to her? Was she pregnant?

The time was ten at night. People in Lagos did not fancy going out and staying out too late because of the fear of armed robbers. How Lagos had changed! In those days when Amaka was schooling in Lagos, the city was a safe place. The war came and everything changed, changed for the worse. People murdered at will. A lot had gone wrong in society.

Father Mclaid was restless, so he drove to Amaka's place. Was something wrong? Had she found somebody else and wanted to ditch him? He knew she was no longer seeing the Alhaji, but was she seeing another person? An officer? Why, why had he at this time of his life fallen in love so helplessly with this middle-aged woman? Was there an explanation?

He had the key to the house. He opened the door, hesitated, then went into the bedroom. Amaka was kneeling in prayer. 'My God,' he whispered and knelt beside her. He said a Hail Mary, prayed with her in his heart and sat down beside her. He was bent on spending the night with her for the first time in their relationship.

'You have come. I thought of phoning but restrained myself, and now you are here. Our minds were working together. Izu, I am pregnant, and you are the father, and I am happy. But . . .I have been praying that God should

103

forgive me for tempting you in this way. I am aware of the havoc I have caused you. As I told you when we first met, I had been declared barren by doctors. I did not use you to get a baby, how could I? I came to you to use you to get contract jobs, and now this, and . . .'

'Darling Amaka, I knew what I was doing. You did not use me, I rather used you. I have no regrets. The baby must be born. I am responsible. All I ask is that you keep this secret until I sort things out. Nothing has changed. I shall continue to take care of you. There are times in one's life when one is left with a choice. This is the time in my life and . . .'

'Izu, I am thirty-two years old and divorced. I am not a teenager who has got into trouble. You don't have to do anything to make me respectable or anything like that. Do you know what it is for me to get pregnant? I would have gone to a beggar in the street if he could make me pregnant. Do you know what it is for gynaecologists to declare you barren, and years after this to find you are pregnant? So I shall carry my pregnancy with pride. It is already four months and has been well established by my doctor. You can see me,' and she stripped for him to see. 'Only I have been warned not to have sex at all, and to have rest, plenty of rest.

'Next week my mother will come and I shall persuade her to stay until the baby is born. I shall not breathe a word to anyone about us. I am in no way obliged to reveal who the father of my baby is.'

'You have been divorced properly you say?' Izu asked, thinking of the custom in Amaka's village, which stipulated that when a women was not divorced properly, her property and subsequent offspring were those of her husband by right of tradition.

'Yes, I have. My mother-in-law wanted to be funny, but my mother outplayed her. I have been properly divorced. The court proceedings went very well. Obiora did not contest the suit. I am free. But why do you ask?'

'Oh, nothing. I just wanted to know. You never can tell, your former husband might want the child and all that. You know what our people are capable of doing. Also your mother may like to know,' he said.

'I will not tell her. I shall tell no one about us. I have only told God about us and have asked him to forgive me.'

'And God will forgive me? I have the greater sin. I was sworn to celibacy and . . . Perhaps I should ask for a dispensation. I should leave the priesthood before the whole thing comes into the open.'

'But nobody will know.'

'You never can tell.'

They slept together that night and he left in the early hours of the morning. By the time he got home, he had decided what would be his next line of action. He had been doing anthropological research, though not all that seriously. He had made notes. He was interested in the obnoxious customs and traditions that chained his people to ignorance and disease. He was particularly interested in the customs that kept the females in bondage. But his biggest assignment to himself was the issue of twins and the custom that enslaved some people in different societies to perpetual second-class citizenship.

He had read books, he had talked to people and he had started jotting down notes. Then Amaka came into his life and he had pushed this self-imposed task to the background. Amaka did not occupy his time as such, but she dominated his thoughts, and that was the crux of the matter. He did not spend much time with her, but he had her in his thoughts every moment of the day.

If he could convince the Bishop to grant him some leave of absence to go to Dublin and sort out his thoughts, no, write his thesis on the issue of twins, he would buy time to decide what line of action he was to take next. Amaka was now his responsibility, he knew it and he wished it to be so, but . . .

Luck was on his side. The Bishop had always liked him. He was one of his best young priests, very much liked by all the older white priests because of his connection with his adoptive father, whom they all respected. And besides, no one had ever said an unkind word against this gentleman. Yes, several young Nigerian priests were not behaving as they should. Many went out in mufti and got drunk in pubs, and got mixed up with girls. Rev. Father Mclaid was not one of them.

But then the Church as a whole was lax in the morals of its own people. An action that would have sent a priest packing was condoned in these days. There was the case of a young priest who was so involved in girls that the women of his parish had to demonstrate against his continued stay there. But nothing was done about it.

The Bishop granted Father Mclaid his request. When he told Amaka, she thought it was a brilliant idea. There would be no gossip at all, and when he came back, everybody would have forgotten her and her baby.

Meanwhile, Amaka's mother had come from Onitsha. At first she said she was not coming because she was very busy. It was almost Christmas and the peak of business. Did Amaka not wish her well by sending her a frantic message to leave her business and take a joyride to Lagos? It was Ayo who had to go and fetch her. 'Come, Mother, Amaka is expecting a baby.'

That did it. When she saw Amaka, she knelt down on the carpeted floor and thanked God:

'God I thank you
God I thank you
With my whole heart
With my whole soul
With my everything.

Didn't I say that
God was kind to me?
God I thank you.

'Amaka get up and let me see you. My daughter, my daughter, so it has happened. My enemies are confounded. Miserable poverty-stricken enemies who trifled with my daughter. Do not be afraid, I am here. Nothing will happen to you. Amaka, so you can look as fresh as this? I have never known my daughter look so well. Where is your maid? Call her, ask her to bring a bottle of schnapps in my basket. That's it,' and she opened it and poured libations. She knelt down and thanked God again.

It was after then that Amaka telephoned Adaobi and invited herself and her mother to her house.

'Of course, Amaka. It's been a long time, and you know how busy I am. The building is progressing very well,' she said over the telephone.

Yes, the building. She was putting up a bungalow in Ikeja on the plot of land she bought without saying a word to her husband. Amaka had helped her do one or two contract jobs she got herself and they had shared the profit. She had even borrowed money from the bank to start, and still owed the bank. She was surprised that she hadn't seen Amaka for so long. But then Lagos was a big place, that was its attraction. One got swallowed up in Lagos. One did whatever one wanted to do in Lagos without anyone interfering.

Amaka and her mother were at Adaobi's house and she was surprised at Amaka. She embraced her gleefully and called her husband to come and see Amaka.

'When did this happen, Amaka? You wonderful girl, so you are not barren after all. Mama Amaka, welcome to Lagos. God has done wonders for my friend.'

'May God's name be praised, my daughter. God has wiped away my daughter's tears, God has glorified my daughter. Enemies are ashamed. God will be with my daughter and she will have the baby in peace.'

'Amen,' they said.

But Mike, Adaobi's husband, did not show such pleasure. He was rather cold about it all. The women noiticed it. Amaka's mother wanted to say something but Amaka pinched her and she was quiet.

When they were gone, Adaobi challenged her husband. 'You men and your hypocrisy! Why did you behave in that atrocious manner? Why should you turn a blessing to shame?'

'Who is the father? Is she going to have a bastard?'

'Meaning the baby would be illegitimate? The word is not in the dictionary of any woman who has not been fortunate to have a husband. All that matters to Amaka and all of us who know her is that she is pregnant. A beggar or a labourer is a man – only a man can make a woman pregnant. Amaka is pregnant, may God help her. She will have her baby in peace.'

'She is going to have her baby out of wedlock. It is a mortal sin . . .'

'Punishable by God in the next world,' Adaobi interrupted. 'Amaka wants to be fulfilled in this world first. Oh my God, Mike, how can you behave like that to my friend? Is she a teenager? A woman who has suffered so much at the hands of men like you has now found happiness and rather than sympathise and wish her well, you behave in this way. Even a priest could not behave in the way you have done. A priest would understand. Even our Mclaid would understand and . . .'

Mike began to laugh. 'Rev. Fr. Mclaid? Will he understand? How nice if he understands. He is the ladies' man . . .' And he laughed on and on. Adaobi was hurt and for days she did not speak to her husband. She cooked for him all right, but she refused to eat with him. A day did not pass without her phoning Amaka to find out how

108

she was getting on. She mothered her and petted her, and looked forward to the day she would have her baby.

Chapter 10

'Mother, when will the doctor open the door for Auntie Amaka's baby to come out?' That was Ayo's youngest child who was excited like everyone else around Amaka. Ayo was greatly amused.

'I don't know that the doctor will have to open the door to let the baby out,' she said to her three year old son.

'So Funke said to me yesterday. She said that the doctor would have to open the belly and let the baby out. Funke said her mother told her.'

'Did she?' Ayo said absentmindedly. She was not very happy with her Permanent Secretary boyfriend of late, whose four children she was looking after. It was not his attention that she cared for, it was the money to take care of the children. He hadn't kept his promise and he had explained to Ayo that things were rather tight, and that the political climate of the country was not what it used to be. But Ayo refused to understand and spent money so recklessly that her boyfriend had to use threats and actually curtail her allowance.

And there was her son telling her what Funke had said. Funke's mother had some relationship with her boyfriend's wife. And it was through her that her boyfriend got to know how she lived. She hated Funke's mother but there was nothing she could do. She could not leave her home because Funke's mother was her neighbour and she could not stop her own children from playing with her avowed enemy, so she lived with the problem. But she refused to change her life-style, which she said was first and foremost encouraged

110

by her boyfriend. It was not easy to begin now to economise. That was a word that was not in her dictionary.

'What else did Funke tell you?' she asked her son.

'Oh, that Auntie Amaka was too old to have a baby And . . . Oh, Mother, I have forgotten what she said. Let's go and see Auntie Amaka today. I want to see Big Mama as well.'

There was no one in when they arrived at Amaka's home, not even the Nanny. So Ayo drove straight to the hospital and almost bumped into her mother.

'Ayo, thanks be to God. Amaka has done it. Two boys, two healthy boys. Thanks be to God. That doctor was good. But why, why didn't we see you yesterday?'

Ayo did not hear. She went straight to Amaka, who had of course not regained consciousness after the operation. The nurses would not let her see the twins.

'Twins, two boys! I can't believe it. I just can't believe it. Amaka has had twins, identical twins. God is merciful. God works in a mysterious way, his wonders to perform.

'Can I see them nurse. I want to see them. My sister's twins. Please nurse,' Ayo begged. So the nurse took her to see the babies. There her mother joined her, and they thanked God again and again.

'My enemies are confounded,' Amaka's mother said. 'I know it. I believed it. I believed that my daughter was not barren. I prayed and hoped. I begged our ancestors and they heard me. God, I thank you with all my heart.'

They drove home and Ayo prepared some pepper soup. Nanny was asked to remain in the hospital, so that when Amaka regained consciousness, it would not be altogether too strange for her. For Amaka had had no labour pains at all, and she was overdue. When the doctor came to see her, she discovered that her blood pressure had risen so high that she took her in her own car to the hospital, and within an hour did a perfect Caesarian operation. She was an experienced gynaecologist and did not take chances. She was a mother of four herself and all four babies were delivered by operations. She was the right doctor for Amaka and she really took care of her. She left as soon as she saw that everything was well, and came back when she thought Amaka would regain consciousness. She sat by her bed and called her name. She opened her eyes and was dazed. Then it appeared she remembered where she was, and looked enquiringly at the doctor, who took her hand and said, 'Congratulations. You have done it. Twins, two boys . . .'

Amaka looked at the doctor in utter confusion.

'Yes, you have done it. Two lovely boys,' the doctor said, still holding her hand. Amaka closed her eyes, then opened them again. She saw the doctor all right. By this time, the dutiful Nanny had come in, and Amaka saw her as well. So she was not dreaming. She called Nanny to make sure that she was the one. She looked at the good doctor. She was not an emotional woman. She still felt the pain of the operation. She noticed that she was breathing fast. She took hold of the doctor's hand and placed it on her chest.

'I feel some emptiness,' she said.

'You will be all right,' the doctor said and rang the bell and a nurse came in. 'Bring the twins for her to see,' she said. 'As far as she is concerned, we are talking in riddles.'

Amaka beckoned to the Nanny. She came but she said nothing to her. She held her hand. Then two nurses brought in the twins.

'They are mine, doctor, the twins are mine. Are you sure? Are they human? Are they all right? My, are you sure, are you . . .'

'Leave her to sleep. I shall come again. The joy is too much for her. She will be all right,' the doctor told the nurses. 'Can you believe it,' she went on, 'that this woman was declared barren many years ago? No, I didn't treat her. She had given up, resigned herself to her fate, and then became pregnant.

She did not even know she was pregnant, not having had the experience before, until we did the urine test, and she registered at the hospital.

'Take care of her. I shall come again to see her. Phone if there is any development.'

But everything went well with Amaka. She remained in the hospital for ten days and went home. There was jubilation. Her mother forgot her business in Onitsha and stayed on, summoning all her children to come and see Amaka and her twin boys.

Adaobi was beside herself with joy and happiness. Mike was not hostile any more. Human lives were now involved. They were there in flesh and blood. Nobody talked of their illegitimacy. And, of course, Adaobi made it clear to Mike that she was not to hear any more nonsense from him. So Mike was careful in conversations about Amaka and her twins.

As soon as Amaka felt strong, her mother took her and the twins home. Ayo was the only one of her children who was free to go with her. They all went by plane to Benin and by road to Onitsha. The purpose of the trip was of course to announce the twins, to show off to home people and to make a big feast, inviting everybody in the village. A cow was slaughtered and those invited and those not invited came and ate and made merry. Food was abundant. When one entertained home people, one must have too much food. People would eat and throw away food. If no food was thrown away, then the host or hostess did not cook enough. Greedy ones had a feast day. They had as many helpings as they cared to have. Amaka's mother saw to that. She, with the women she had picked, did the cooking and organised the crowd. As a result, nobody grumbled. Those who came purposely to find fault went away disappointed, but of course they had something to say when they got to their homes. 'Oh, we saw the twins all right. Are you sure they

113

were hers?' one incredulous woman asked.

'There is no end to what Amaka and her mother could do,' another said.

'If the twins are not hers, whose are they? She did not pick them up from the streets of Lagos. She did not steal them either. Didn't you see Amaka and how she looked? You are a mother. Didn't you see that she looked like one who was nursing babies?'

'It's the mystery of the father that baffles everyone including Amaka's own people. Whoever the father was should have graced the occasion whether he is a married man or not. For I heard it whispered that the father could not come because he is married and in the civil service.'

'That story is not true. They are confusing Ayo with Amaka.'

'But that family is quite something. They beat everyone. Mama Amaka must be a happy woman having such wonderful and lucky children. All her children have made it. Amaka, whom everyone thought was going to end up childless and husbandless, now has children, two boys at a go.'

'They are lucky. In the olden days, she would not have set eyes on the twins. They would have been killed and the gods and goddesses of the land appeased.'

'That was over seventy years ago.'

'No, ten years ago. Some people still throw away twins.'

'Ten years ago?'

'Of course. As a matter of fact, I was told by my aunt, who was a nursing sister with the mission, that in some parts of Enugu area, that pregnant mothers, for fear of having twins, went to the bush to have their babies all by themselves. If they had twins, they took one and did away with the other. The mission knew about this and so the converts in that area kept watch. Whenever there was a hint, they saved the twins. And, as a result, the local people were antagonistic to the mission. She knew of a particular case in which twins were saved and were adopted by a priest.'

People talked and talked. But what intrigued many most was the attitude of Amaka's mother-in-law, who was present and claimed that the twins belonged to her son. She unashamedly said so to everyone. She ate all that was served and drank a bit too much. It was rather embarrassing for Amaka and Ayo particularly. But their mother was equal to the task.

'Leave her alone. Let her talk. You are not the only ones hearing her. Make sure you serve her all she asks for and even more. Her son knows better than she does, so take no notice of what she says. Do you see her son here? He is in town but you will not find him here.'

Obiora was indeed not there. He was most unhappy about his break with his wife which was, of course, caused by his mother. There was nothing he could do other than make up with the woman who bore him two sons. The woman did not know her right from her left, and what was worse, did not acknowledge the fact. She behaved atrociously and embarrassed Obiora. But he could do nothing about her. He had taken his problem philosophically. He was getting on and if he dared cause anything that would disrupt the relationship he would be in the soup. He would have no family at all, and he would be a laughing-stock in the presence of his friends, age-grade and colleagues. So he stuck to this woman whom he refused to marry conventionally.

Obiora had thought of seeing Amaka before she went back to Lagos, at least for old times' sake. But he was shy by nature and so found it rather difficult to go. Amaka, on the other hand, wanted to see her ex-husband, to see whether he had aged as they told her and of course to show off her new-found wealth which she exhibited according to the dictates of the time.

Amaka wore no abada materials any more, but lace and

115

'jorge' even in the kitchen. She wore nothing but gold and coral beads, and she always had everything to match no matter whether she was at home or at her site or at church.

But what really impressed people was that she gave generously. And so relatives and friends poured in and she gave them money, raw cash. The people wondered. Did she have a mint? Did she break into a bank? Was her husband, or rather the father of her twins, a top army officer or even the General himself? They speculated, they gossiped, yet they came to her, told her their problems and she gave them money.

Her mother was happy that she could afford the money to give to both her friends and even her enemies. 'You are making sacrifices, my daughter,' she said to her. 'I hear all the gossip. Those who say nasty things about you are the very people who come to you with their monetary problems. So I say help wherever you can and God will reward you a hundredfold.'

Their people believed that once God gave you wealth that you must share it with your relatives and in fact the whole village. The whole village had a right to your wealth, because anybody among them could have had that wealth instead of you. Therefore, you must give generously and you were severely criticised if you did not. If suddenly you lost all your fortune out of stupidity or neglect or a wrong economic decision, nobody rallied round to commiserate with you. All and sundry gave unfavourable reasons for your misfortune and laughed at you behind your back.

Amaka's mother told her that she was a lucky woman. The kind of wealth she had was not bestowed on women at all, but men. Those women who made great fortunes in their village when Amaka's mother was only a girl were childless. Wealth came first, and blocked the chances of having children. According to their belief, the two did not go together. You either had children or you had wealth. Her

116

own daughter had disproved this belief. She now had two lovely sons and wealth. What could be better than that? She was very proud of her daughter and rightly so. Who wouldn't be?

So Amaka continued to give, until she was ready to go back to Lagos. She was already starting a building of her own in her village and had given her mother the necessary funds for it. For she knew that when she came home again, she had to stay in her own house and not depend entirely on her mother for accommodation.

Again she thought of seeing Obiora. Surely she still felt something for the man who had been her husband for more than six years. She was in a position of strength now, with money and children. So she should be magnanimous and make the first move. She told her mother, who did not see why she should, but raised no objection. Ayo did not like the idea at all.

'They are all the same, Amaka, these men. Tell me why you want to see him? A man who virtually drove you out of your home because you did not have a child for him! And besides, you have divorced him both in our native law and custom and in the law courts. Again, there is one thing you have not given a thought to yet – and that is the father of your boys. You have not told us anything about him Mother and I do not know who this lucky man is, and we have been waiting for you to tell us . . .'

'Just speak for youself,' Amaka's mother cut in. 'Whoever is the father of the twins is a man. Why do we want to know who he is now? Amaka will tell us if she wants to, but we are not to bring it up at all. Amaka is a woman, she is a mother, and that's all that matters right now. I don't want to know what our people are saying about the father of the twins. My daughter is a mother, and if Amaka wants to see Obiora again, by all means let her see him. What do you think, Ayo? I thought you were like me. Do you think Amaka would ever

117

go back to that miserable husband of hers again after the divorce? No, she won't. She is curious, that's all, and I can understand her curiosity. You have done perfectly well without a husband these long years, and you still depend, so to say, on the father of your children. Amaka has made it and without a husband. She will pull through. Do you think she is going to get on well, do her business well, if she has to look after a husband. Oh, no, she can't. She would either have a husband or her business, she could not have both. The demands of her husband would be too much and she would be unable to cope.

'What do you children think was the reason why our prosperous mothers went out of their way to marry wives for their husbands? They were wise. They did not want to sacrifice their trade or economic life by waiting on husbands and ministering to their every need. So our mothers got young wives who did these soul-destroying chores for their husbands while they themselves concentrated on their trade.

'Your sister, Ayo, has passed this stage. She is learning to be like you. She is discovering what it is to be independent. She is discovering what it is to have wealth, she wouldn't sacrifice that for any man even if he were a top army officer or a millionaire.'

It was after this argument that Amaka's mother asked Obiora to come and see Amaka and her twins. Obiora came, bringing his own boys. It was not a bad meeting. Obiora had aged a good deal and was not the handsome man Amaka had known. People change so much. It was only three years ago that she left Obiora, and a lot had happened in those three years. It surprised both of them that they had nothing to say to each other after the first pleasantries. Amaka was not even sure what had motivated her desire to see her ex-husband. Obiora felt so inadequate to talk to her. Amaka's wealth was everywhere for him to see, and it embarrassed him. But Amaka's mother was there to save the situation. She talked of nothing in particular, but she went on yapping. How nice it was to see Obiora in her house. Why was he unable to come to the party thrown by Amaka, when his mother came and thoroughly enjoyed herself? Why did he not come to see them with his wife? Then she commented on his healthy-looking sons, adding that their mother must be a wonderful mother.

Amaka said nothing. She was thoughtful as her mother went on and on without stopping. Was this man the husband with whom she had lived for six years? She felt nothing for him any more. He could drop dead now, she would be sorry, but that was all. Was this the man she begged to let her be his wife even if he wanted to marry twenty wives? Was this man the man she loved so much and married? Why did she feel nothing towards him any more?

Was it time? Was it Izu, the father of her twins? Was it her new position of wealth? The life she lived in Lagos? The discovery that she, rejected by her own husband, was attractive to other men in Lagos who were in positions of wealth and influence?

She did not regret anything. Surely, God's time was the best. The day broke for different people at different times, according to the saying of her people. For her day broke three years ago, three short years in which God gave her wealth and children and a man to love and to cherish.

She hadn't told the priest about the birth of the twins. He had asked her not to send word about the birth or anything concerning them both. Ayo was right to bring up the question. At least her mother and Ayo should know who the father of her twins was. How was she going to break the news to them? How were they going to take it, that a priest was the father of her children? Her mother was not a professed Christian, but Amaka felt that she was going to be shocked all the same. She was not sure about Ayo, but she was sure about how her other sisters and brothers would feel. Then, of course, there were the village people. It would be the talk of the village for a long time to come.

What would Adaobi think? She was understanding, but she was sure she would die of embarrassment. She refused to think of Adaobi's husband and his reaction when they learnt the truth. It was then that she began to think of Izu and his next line of action. Of course she was sure that he was not going to claim the twins. In that case, she would bring them up playing the role of father and mother. This role excited her. There would be no one to dictate to her, to tell her what she should do and what she should not do. She would bring up her children well. She would not pet them. She would love them and minister to their every need.

It did not occur to her that perhaps Izu might make some demands of her. Was it the excitement of the past three months or what? Did she really feel anything for Izu? She was not sure. She knew for sure that she had not missed him even before the babies were born. What was wrong with her? Was she not capable of loving anyone any more. Was she so mercenary that nothing mattered except naira and kobo? What had happened to her these three years in Lagos? She loved her twins. She loved her mother, her sisters and brothers. She felt nothing for the Alhaji, for the others who came after him. And right now she was searching herself to see whether she felt anything for Izu, the father of her twins, the man who proved to the world that she was capable of bearing children. She was grateful to him, grateful for the contracts that she got through him. Grateful for the love he showed for her, for the care, but did she love him? If she had loved him, she would not have had these thoughts. She did not love him. That was what it boiled down to. And she did not even want to love anybody except her twins and her relations. In that way she reasoned, one avoided being hurt. She did not realise how hurt she was until her eyes were opened in Lagos and she began to see what she could do as a woman, using her bottom power, as they say in Nigeria.

How was she going to face Izu if and when he came back? Could he have run away? From her? No, that thought was rather unkind of her. She knew that Izu was genuine. She knew and understood why he had to leave Lagos for Dublin.

What she did not know was what Izu's reaction would be when he came back from Dublin and saw the twins.

Chapter 11

Rev. Father Mclaid came back to Lagos unexpectedly. Someone very important in government had sent an urgent message to him asking him to return. The message was not clear, but he could not ignore it. As a matter of fact, he had become restless, and had not done much in his research. He had calculated when Amaka was due, and it was from then on that he felt lonely and restive as well.

So it was a welcome message coming from the man, so important and so much attached to the Bishop he worked under. He had heard no news at all about the twins. It was agreed that Amaka should seal her lips and should send no messages or letters of any kind.

He went straight to see the Bishop who welcomed him very well and asked him about his studies and research. Then he took him in and told him about the change that was about to take place in Nigeria shortly. He was not very sure of the event he spoke about, but he was in agreement that Father Mclaid should return and be available at any time.

Even the man in government who asked the priest to return was not sure of what was about to happen. He did not pretend to know. All he told him was that there was a persistent rumour that there was going to be a change in government. Whether it was going to be bloodless or not, he was not sure. The reverend gentleman, who was the Chaplain and quite high in government, would have to go. He was not sure how he was to be disposed of though. He was sure that if the event took place at all, that he would go and Father Mclaid would step into his shoes. The man in government had worked all that out. He wanted his own man in the position of influence. He had nothing against the incumbent, but he did not feel relaxed dealing with him, and that was why Father Mclaid was sent for.

Father Mclaid's background was not known to many people. Even his fellow priests thought he was not a Nigerian. Only a handful of Irish priests and of course the Bishop knew where he came from and how he came about that name. The influential man in government did not know either. He had liked him and his sermons, but had never associated him with the East and its dynamic and 'strange' people. The influential man was rather vague and Father Mclaid wondered about the reason for his summons to Lagos in the first place. However, after the briefing, as he referred humourously to his order to come back, he went to see Amaka, who was of course not expecting him. He had brought no presents. It was awkward for him to bring feminine and infant presents back to Nigeria. His heart was beating as he drove to Amaka's residence. As usual, it was at night, and he had the key to the back door, which he found bolted from the inside. That was understandable. He had been away for nearly a year, and Amaka was afraid of armed robbers. It was ten o'clock, and he could hear voices, feminine voices, thank God. So he knocked and the door was opened by Nanny, who had one of the twins in her arms.

'Oh, Father!' Nanny shouted and knelt down.

'Please get up,' Father Mclaid said, and took the baby from her arms. In the bedroom were Amaka and her sister Ayo. They had the latest 'jorge' material spread on the floor. The name of the 'jorge' was 'Rolls Royce' and it cost only five hundred naira for a piece which was just enough for what one wanted. There were some pieces of lace and a headtie to match the 'jorge' and they cost just three hundred and one hundred and fifty naira each respectively. They were discussing quietly the effect the lace and the headtie would

123

have on the 'jorge' and so did not hear the knock on the door. The other twin was sleeping and Nanny was just about to put the other twin boy in his cot when she heard the knock.

Father Mclaid controlled himself very well when Nanny asked him to sit in the sitting room while she called her mistress. His urge was to go straight to the bedroom. He sat down and looked at the sleeping baby and all fatherly instincts were aroused in him. 'This is my baby,' he said, 'this is mine and mine alone. Oh, God forgive me. But this is my baby . . .'

Ayo was the first to come out of the bedroom. When she saw Father Mclaid with the baby, she deduced intuitively that he was the father of the twins. She needed no confession from her sister. It was only a father who could carry a baby like that. She was a mother herself and she knew when her boyfriend came in the dead of night to see her and his children. She knew the way he carried the babies which were his. She wanted to be light-hearted about it, and to use the biblical sentence: 'Thou art the man,' but she restrained herself. After all, she was not familiar with Father Mclaid. She had heard about him, casually referred to as a very nice man who helped people and who preached very good sermons. She had never associated him with her sister. It was a secret Amaka kept to herself almost under pain of death.

Then Amaka came out of the bedroom carrying the other baby, who was awake for no reason at all. It was simply too much for Father Mclaid. The secret was out. 'Amaka, you had twins. I am a twin myself. Oh my God, my twins, both boys. I cannot believe it.' He embraced Amaka.

'Why not? You are a twin. That's what it should be. Twins beget twins. Ayo, that's the father of the boys.'

Nanny was somewhere around. She had known for a long time so it did not come as a surprise to her at all. Her mistress was only confirming what she had already known as soon as it was established that she was pregnant.

It did not seem real at all to Father Mclaid. It was like a pleasant dream. He would wake up and find that he was still in Dublin doing his research on female circumcision, and thinking of Amaka and Nigeria.

'I had to return,' he said, when Amaka showed surprise at his sudden return. 'I was actually summoned. I came back two days ago. Have you anything for me to eat?'

Nanny went straight to the kitchen and prepared some food very fast. Meanwhile Ayo took her leave.

As soon as they were alone, Izu began, 'I have to leave the priesthood.' Amaka thought she had not heard properly and said, 'I beg your pardon?' Izu hesitated before he repeated what he had said. He did not like Amaka's tone. There was a mild irritation in her voice.

'How did it go in Dublin? I hope you had a nice time. All those lovely Irish nuns and . . .'

Izu was deeply hurt. 'Amaka,' he almost shouted. That was the first time he had ever raised his voice talking to Amaka. That was the first time Amaka saw him really angry. Was she playing with fire and she did not know it? However, whatever it was, she had her twins. If the worst came to the worst, she would produce a father for the twins. She was surprised at her own thoughts.

'Now, listen to me,' he said, as if reading her thoughts. 'The twins are mine and I am going to claim them, and no power in this world will stop me. And before I claim them, I am going to leave the priesthood. I am seeing the Bishop tomorrow for dispensation. I shall confess all to him, and I am positive he will be sympathetic.'

Amaka was taken aback. She never for one moment thought that Izu would feel that way towards the twins. She was frightened and found herself the next morning at her sister's. Ayo was preparing her last-born for school when

125

Amaka drove in and sat on her bed, feeling a bit off-colour. Ayo smiled at her and continued dressing the child. Then she sent him to the dining room and sat on the chair waiting for her sister to begin.

'Izu,' she stammered. 'He wants the twins.'

'Naturally,' Ayo said. 'He is a Nigerian isn't he? Nigerian men fight tooth and nail for their offspring, no matter whether they have twenty. Did you think he was going to deny that he was the father? You haven't begun yet to understand the Nigerian male. What bothers you anyway? You have your twins. You have now proved you can be a mother. Father Mclaid is a man first and foremost. Didn't you know that before they were allowed to join the priesthood, they had to be subjected to a test to show that they could perform like any other men. And . . .'

Amaka could not help smiling in spite of herself.

'Yes,' her sister went on, 'they had to be tested so that they did not cheat in any way and . . .'

'How do you mean cheat?' asked Amaka.

'Well, simple. A man might know he could not perform and to save himself any embarrassment join the priesthood,' she said.

'Many join when they are boys and very innocent.'

'Yes, but when do they take their vows? However, be that as it may, you have a problem. Your twins must have a name, and you don't want to use your ex-husband's.'

'God forbid. I wanted to use our father's name. It is done, even now.'

'I know, but this case is different.'

'I know, Ayo, but think of the gossip, the problems involved. Think of poor Father Mclaid.'

'Your lover does not think himself all that poor, my sister. He is excited, and as I see him, he would move heaven and earth to have his twins. The priesthood is not what it used to be when we were girls. A lot has changed. Nuns found themselves pregnant during the war. Priests had lovers who bore them children and some of them are still priests today. Others decided to quit the priesthood.'

'That's why Izu's outburst frightens me. I thought he was going to shy away from it all. I never thought, knowing his background, that he would want to be associated with any children that resulted from our affair. And what really bothers me is that he wants me and the twins. I don't want him. I don't want to be his wife. I think he is realising it, and wants to have the twins for a start. Ayo, I don't want to be a wife any more, a mistress yes, with a lover, yes of course, but not a wife. There is something in that word that does not suit me. As a wife, I am never free. I am a shadow of myself. As a wife I am almost impotent. I am in prison, unable to advance in body and soul. Something gets hold of me as a wife and destroys me. When I rid myself of Obiora, things started working for me. I don't want to go back to my "wifely" days. No, I am through with husbands. I said farewell to husbands the first day I came to Lagos.'

And she began to cry. But Ayo was a seasoned Lagos woman who did not see why Amaka should feel the way she was feeling.

'Don't behave that way,' she said. 'Why, Izu has not even said he wants to marry you. I don't see your problem, Amaka. I have four children without a husband and I am happy. Perhaps you are being involved with Izu. Otherwise, why should you talk in the way you are now talking. I find your attitude rather strange. Does your good friend know about Izu?' she asked finally.

'I have not told her. I have kept it a secret. Adaobi must think it is the Alhaji. I wonder what she would feel if I told her.'

'Well, don't tell her. Try and sort yourself out first. You never can tell what her reaction will be. How is your business going?'

'Very well.'

'I have not told you that there is a rumour about a possible change in government. So I am preparing myself and the children. You get prepared too. Have you enough money on you? We don't know the form it will take. Some say it will be bloody, others say it will not. Whether bloody or bloodless, all of us are going to be affected. Get mother to finish building your house quickly in case of any emergency. Get yourself properly organised. I am thinking of taking the children to London. We have a house there. I want to be there before my number one. You can see how practical I am. No nonsense. Think less of Izu and more of yourself and the twins. And bear in mind that Izu can take care of himself, but the twins cannot. So they come first.'

'Oh, I have ruined Izu's career. How can he leave the priesthood for my sake?'

'Men have been known to leave their thrones for their women. But those were spineless men. How I used to admire that prince who left his throne for a divorced woman. But now I see that he was stupid. My, in this world he could have married one out of a hundred princesses and yet be happy. Don't worry. Izu is sensible. You have not ruined his career. He wants to opt out of the priesthood. He is tired of it. He is only using you. And I want you to bear in mind that you are not going to be happy with him if you ever marry him. The world he would be introduced to would be too exciting for him. He would be free to meet younger women and would want to sleep with them. He would discover the difference and there and then your troubles would start. So I agree with you that you should not marry him when he proposes, that is if he does propose. I tell you that he is using you. If he did not want to opt out of the priesthood, he would lie low and nobody would ever associate you with him.'

'You now know and Nanny knows.'

'I can keep your secret, and knowing Nanny as I do, she too will keep it.

128

'Listen, listen to the radio. There is an announcement. The government has been overthrown by a group of army officers. I don't know what he calls himself, my God,' Amaka said.

Amaka and Ayo listened as the broadcast was repeated. Gowon had been overthrown. Amaka and Ayo began to cry. They liked Gowon. He saved their people. Without him, the Ibos would have been slaughtered like sheep and goats at the end of the civil war.

'Ayo, I must go back to my children. Give me a ring if you hear any further news.'

And with this coup, things began to change, and to change fast for everyone. There was jubilation, as usual, heralding the coup plotters who were for the moment heroes. A lot was said about the fall of Gowon's government. The military governors who were almost worshipped, turned into public enemies. They were found guilty of one thing or another. Few gave them credit for what they did or what they failed to do. Journalists had their field day writing their jargon as usual. What was more, the man who rose to be the Head of State was almost regarded as a god.

The axe fell on both small and great. There came massive retirements from the army and the civil service, and Father Mclaid was elevated, through the influential politician, to the post of Commissioner in the Federal Republic of Nigeria. He had no portfolio as such but he was a member of the Federal Executive Council, and being a good man and a priest, his influence was wide.

Adaobi nearly swooned when she heard of Father Mclaid's new position and doubled her efforts in building the bungalow, without the knowledge of her husband. Mike did not feel what his wife felt. He was a dutiful officer who had done no wrong to anyone, so why should the change affect him? But the change did affect him in a most painful way. He was working late in his office. The new regime wanted to do

129

everything at once. It looked as if the devil himself was after them and urged them on to disrupt society, dislodge people from their homes and cause sadness and fear throughout. They demanded information right, left and centre in forty-eight hours or with immediate effect. Before one got the demanded information, they had forgotten it and demanded more. Poor civil servants who took their work seriously were badly harrassed.

Poor Mike was slow but efficient. It was because of his slowness that he was spending extra hours in the office when his wife phoned him and asked him to come home immediately.

'But, Adaobi, please be reasonable. I have to submit this paper tomorrow to my commissioner at ten, and I cannot afford the luxury of my home now . . .'

'Mike, do you hear me? Come home immediately or they will come and get you.' That was serious. So he left his office, the paper he was writing and the files on the table, and picked up his briefcase. He shut the office and asked the messenger who was on duty to lock the door.

As soon as he was out of earshot, the messenger had a good laugh. 'Dis government na war. Oga no no say they done sack am with immediate effect.'

'Una dey laugh?' another messenger joined in. 'Why una dey laugh? Una don see government we sack judge? Make una wait, na kill they go kill una, no bi sack.'

'Oga messenger, I hear you,' another went on. 'Dis government no dey sack people we do nothing. Na people we do someting. Na people we do someting na them dis government de sack, you hear? Papa Gowon, you hear.'

Mike could not believe what he saw when he arrived home. His neighbours were all in the sitting room looking gloomy. He thought he had lost his child or all his children. It was a neighbour whom he had hardly spoken to in the last four years, who told him that it had just been announced

130

over the radio that he and his Permanent Secretary, together with his Director, had been sacked with immediate effect. And that he was given forty-eight hours to move from his official residence. It was then that he sat down and stared into space.

Then he got up and went into the room and called his wife. 'Have you phoned Father Mclaid?'

'I haven't. The news came barely half an hour ago.'

'Let's go and see him then. He can do something. I think it is a mistake. There are two or three of us bearing the same name. It could not be me. How can I be retired with immediate effect? Let's go and see him.'

'Let's phone first.' And Adaobi, visibly shaken, dialled Father Mclaid's home. Someone answered and told her that he was not in and it was most unlikely he would return that night, and hung up rather rudely.

They tried again when the neighbours left them, but there was no answer. Then it occured to Adaobi that she should phone her friend, Amaka. She had, of course, rejoiced with her about her twins and made clothes for them. But she was not interested in the paternity of them, or rather she felt that if her friend wanted her to know, she would tell her voluntarily.

The telephone was engaged and she decided to drive all the way, not minding the situation in Lagos and the traffic jams. In no time at all, she was at her friend's, knocking on the door and Nanny, ever present, opened it. The first person she saw was Father Mclaid carrying one of the boys.

'Congratulations,' Adaobi said to him. 'Mike and I have tried to reach you as soon as we heard the news, but then you were so busy. Even this evening, I tried several times to get your home, but failed. How are you? I am delighted at your new position.'

Amaka came out and embraced her friend and took her by the hand to the bedroom. 'I am happy you have come. I

131

wanted to call you when I heard the news this evening, but I was not sure whether it was your Mike or some other Mike. Is it true?'

Adaobi nodded, tears filling her eyes.

'Did you manage to complete the bungalow?'

'Not quite. I have the doors to hang and other little things that take a lot of time.'

'I have my workers. They can help. But there is something I have been unable to tell you, Adaobi. I didn't have the courage. But I know that I must tell you. Father Mclaid is the father of my twins . . .'

'Is what?' Perhaps she did not quite hear her. Perhaps the events of the day were just too much for her. But she was shocked later at what she told her good friend.

'You Amaka, you of all people. You, how could you tempt a man of God? A priest of God, vowed to be celibate. How could you? I didn't know you could do that. Oh, I am so disappointed in you. Oh, no, no, it is not true. Father, Father . . .' And she ran out of the bedroom. 'Is it true? Is it true?'

'It is true, Adaobi. Don't worry. I have already confessed to the Bishop. He was understanding. I told him it was not easy for me seeing the twins and knowing that they are mine. Look at them. They look like me. There is no denying it. I am sorry, Adaobi, to have disappointed you and your husband and many others. But there is nothing I can do. And this new appointment does help a bit. I can still be useful to the Church and maybe if you could persuade your friend to be my wife, we could arrange things nicely that there would not be too much scandal.'

Adaobi did not know how she reached home that night. She had even forgotten her own plight. Her husband was sitting all by himself in the sitting room when she drove in, and sat down without saying a word.

'Where did you go?' he asked. 'Oh, to see whether the

house had been completed.'

'Which house?'

'The one I am building. It's a bungalow. We shall hang the doors tomorrow and will move in in the evening.'

What had he done that all these things should come to him all at once? What was his wife saying to him? He thought she had gone to see Father Mclaid to complain about his disgrace. Why this? Which house was she talking about? Did Father tell her that it was all a mistake, that they would phone him tomorrow and apologise? Why on earth should he be retired for inefficiency and divided loyalty and drunkenness.

'Listen to me, Mike. I am moving out of this house tomorrow evening. There is nothing Father Mclaid or any other person can do in the circumstances. So the sooner we face reality the better. I got this place about a year ago and have managed to put up something. Amaka helped me a lot. I got contracts and she executed them and we shared the profits. I didn't want to tell you, knowing the way you behave in these matters. So we move tomorrow. As I see it, more will be retired and nobody is going to do anything about it. They say it is a revolution. But how many revolutions is one entitled to in a lifetime? I only hope they won't start shooting one another. If they do, I shall run away with my children.'

She went to the bedroom and began to put her things together. Mike sat in the sitting room. In a matter of some six hours he had aged six years.

Chapter 12

Father Mclaid had a hard time with the Bishop, who was shocked, to put it mildly.

'And, my Lord, I cannot continue as a priest with this knowledge that I have sinned and have abandoned my sons as well. They are like me. There is no way of denying it. Even if I do, my conscience will trouble me. How am I going to live with myself for the rest of my life? I want a clean break. There is no middle way for me.'

The Bishop was at a loss. It was the most painful decision he had had to take in all his forty years as a priest of God and a Bishop. Times had changed, and he had to move with the times. He had to grant Father Mclaid's request. There was nothing else he could do. Mclaid had done what was expected of him: he had come to confess to the Bishop. That was a penance in itself. He must grant him dispensation.

Many young priests, during and after the war had not lived up to expectations. There was so much laxity amongst both priests and nuns. There were many cases like Father Mclaid's but those concerned did not handle their problems the way he had done. They had allowed the scandal to go on, and had only come to the Bishop when it was too late.

There was the case of a priest of God who got involved with a girl during the war. He sent the girl to his mother. She had the baby and lived with the priest's mother in the village while the priest visited her from time to time. By the time it was known, the priest had already had four children and had to leave the priesthood. It was very scandalous, and there were attempts at a cover-up by the Church. But many people knew and the influence of the Church began to diminish. Father Mclaid approached his problem admirably and maturely. Others like him who had fallen by the wayside, invented one excuse or another to leave the priesthood. There was one in particular who made headlines in the newspapers fighting the very institution that he had belonged to over twenty years. It was painful for the others who still believed, for they reasoned, and rightly too, that if one was tired of an organisation or an institution which one had defended for so long, one should leave quietly and not disrupt that very institution. One should not incite others to revolt and cause harm. Father Mclaid and many like him argued in this vein and abhorred the writings and sayings in the news media of their colleagues who, to all intents and purposes, wanted to do what they liked. While in the priesthood, they were not allowed to do as they liked.

So, in this particular case, Amaka's name was never mentioned. Father Mclaid would not grant interviews with anyone, when he was appointed, for he believed that the press boys could ask him embarrassing questions about his life. He wasn't sure that his secret was secret, so he was always on his guard. The Bishop was sorry, but he admired Father Mclaid's courage, knowing his background. He was not just one of the priests, he was an outcast who would have died but for the Church. The good Bishop took note of the other aspects of the young man's transgressions.

Later in the evening of the same day, Father Mclaid went to see Amaka's mother, whom he had sent for to see whether she could persuade Amaka to be his wife as soon as decency allowed. Amaka was reluctant to send the message and had told him that she was not going to change her mind. She cherished the relationship all right, but marriage, no. She was through with it. She might have considered it as a means of having children, but now that she had the twins, there was no way. It was irksome for Father Mclaid to think that he

135

could ask to leave the priesthood, because he was involved with a woman who had his twins, and this same woman refused to be his wife. He had thought that every woman's ambition was to get married, have children and settle down with the man she loved. Amaka was proving difficult, but he would press on.

Before Amaka's mother was sent for, he had already had a session with Ayo, Amaka's sister. Ayo was not happy on that particular day because her boyfriend and her number one had taken off to London without a word . If he had nothing to hide, he would not have gone so unceremoniously. However, no matter. Men were all the same, Ayo had concluded ages ago. As a younger woman she had used men as part of her outfit. She had said that a woman needed a nice man to be by her side when she was properly dressed for an outing, and when one was ready to have children, one needed them for that purpose only – procreation. If they had money to go with it, all well and good.

Father Mclaid was not happy at the outcome of his discussion with Ayo. He had thought that Ayo would be on his side, but Ayo was on her sister's side.

'Father,' she said. 'I beg your pardon, Izu. I don't see you and my sister making a good pair. Let's face it. You are not of this world really. The life you are about to enter is a strange one. There are so many things you do not know yet. You are excited about the twins, who wouldn't be? But think of your profession, your new office, and don't rush things. My sister is very stubborn. She went through hell in her marriage. That hell is still at the back of her mind. Try as much as you can, she cannot forget it. She likes you as a person, but she does not want to get married again. So my advice is this: take it coolly. Get on with your job. Don't be rash. Don't leave the priesthood and things will sort themselves out in due course. That is my advice.'

Father Mclaid did not take the advice, of course. And so

he went to the Bishop and confessed all, believing that once he did that, Amaka would realise how serious he was. But that did not impress Amaka in any way. Next to Ayo was Adaobi. He wanted to see her and bare his heart to her. Somehow he preferred to talk to Adaobi rather than Mike. Nigerian men talked to their fellow men in those circumstances, not to women. Father Mclaid was, of course, ignorant of the way Nigerian men behaved, not having a close friend who was not a priest. As a matter of fact, he had no friends even among his fellow priests. They envied him, because of the preferential treatment he received and his good qualities.

He was not prepared at all for the way Adaobi treated him. Mike was busy writing endless petitions which nobody in government had time to read. Father Mclaid had advised him to lie low, until he sorted things out, but he was impatient. He thought that the injustice done to him would be rectified in a month or so. Adaobi, who was practical, had told him to desist from the petitions. They were all right so far. They had moved to their bungalow, and she still had her job. The children were in school. Their lifestyle hadn't changed drastically. If he would use the days as a holiday and have a good rest, all would be well.

Adaobi found it extremely difficult to be of any use to Father Mclaid. She refused to discuss the matter. Her faith in the Church was so shaken that she would not forgive Father Mclaid. He could be the Head of State tomorrow, for all she cared, but she was not going to change her attitude towards him. He had let her down so badly. As for Amaka, she called her all sorts of names. She seduced the man of God, and she would not go unpunished. She was not going to talk Amaka into marrying Father Mclaid. She could never encourage that kind of marriage. The Father who gave her holy communion, being the father of her best friend's children, no. It was just too much for her to take.

The only person left to talk to was Amaka's mother. And he was driving to Amaka's house, this time in the daytime, to see Amaka's mother. Amaka, Ayo and their mother were waiting for Izu's arrival when Amaka again told them that she had made up her mind and would not marry Izu.

'Mother, she does not love him,' said Ayo in her usual way.

'Who is talking about love now?' their mother said. 'You children got the idea of love into your heads when you went to school and read those books.'

'Mother,' Ayo began almost in jest. 'Don't tell us you did not love our father when you married him.'

'I'll tell you frankly, I had nothing to do at all in the marriage between your father and I. It was my mother who arranged everything. I protested. I said I didn't like him, that I didn't want to marry him, but she said he was a good man and from a very good family. And that she would always be near to me to help me and encourage me. I loved my mother so much that I agreed. In the first ten years of the marriage, I had all of you. But I still did not love him. In fact, as time went on, I disliked him more and more. But I remained his wife. He knew I did not like him, but he was a very patient man. Even when I encouraged him to get another wife, he refused. I felt so guilty, but there was nothing I could do. I told my mother, but she saw nothing in my complaints. She encouraged me to trade. So I went to Onitsha and started trading in textiles.

'I would leave home and not return for two weeks. My husband did not mind. When I asked him to come over to Onitsha and live with me, he refused. He stayed at home and took care of you together with my mother. He loved my mother and she treated him like a real son, for as you know, she had no son.

'Then he died rather prematurely and I was left with my mother to bring you up. I think nothing of him, except that

138

he was the father of my children. There was no affection as such, even when he died, he was no loss to me. This is the truth. So I can understand Amaka. And remember that her own circumstances are quite different from mine. So if she did not feel anything for Izu, I can understand. But Amaka, you should think of Izu's position now. You have his children now and he wants you. You have your own house and are quite independent. Your circumstances have changed drastically. You will be free. You will be financially independent of him. Your previous marriage was different. You were young, you had no money of your own, though you had a business. But now you have two lovely boys. The boys need a father. You could bring them up better if they were girls, but they are boys and they will be quite a handful for you alone. So think of Izu seriously. If you cannot make up your mind now, you can make it up in future, say next year. You have nothing to lose. You have much more to gain.'

Izu drove in and parked in the garage. Amaka's mother welcomed him profusely, and offered kola and drinks which Izu took. He was relaxed among the three women. The twins were in their cots, wide awake. He did not carry them in his arms. He merely went to the cots, smiled at them, and sat down again. Then he began:

'Amaka's mother, I have already told the Bishop about Amaka and myself. I cannot go back and unsay those things again. If Amaka does not want marriage now, she might want it some other time, but she has to make up her mind pretty soon. I am impatient. It has been a difficult decision for me to take, and having taken it, I cannot go back. I have left the priesthood, and what use is this action of mine if Amaka refuses to be my wife. I don't want half-measures. I know of other priests who are involved like me and still remain in the priesthood. Amaka wants me to do that but I cannot do it, because I am different.'

Nobody spoke after he had spoken, not even Amaka's

139

mother. There was a mild threat in his words. And when he was gone, the three women looked at each other blankly. Amaka's mother slept badly. As for Amaka, she slept very well. She had made her decision and that was that.

Early in the morning, Amaka's mother woke her up, and spoke softly to her for over ten minutes about protection by men, about her own life without a husband and all that. Izu was a good man who wanted her desperately and she should consider him. Izu had no one in the way of relations who would bother Amaka if she became his wife. Amaka would be in an enviable position as the wife of a Federal Commissioner. She would have contracts and everyone would bend over backwards to do her will. Amaka should not shy away from marriage because of her previous experiences. Izu was a man of God and would not let her down. He was responsible and Amaka would never regret the marriage.

Amaka listened and when her mother finished, she said nothing, but went to the telephone and called Ayo and asked her to come post haste.

'Just ask Mother why she woke me up at five this morning. Let me say it again, I am through with marriage. I am not going to marry Izu. Have I made myself clear, Mother?'

Amaka's mother's back was up. 'Amaka, who are you talking to in that way? Now listen to me, you stupid ass. Money indeed. How much are you worth? Just tell me and I shall tell you how much I am worth. When I finish with you, then you will know who is your mother. Now listen, listen very carefully to me. You will marry Izu. I will not die until you marry him. So get it straight. Ayo, you are my witness. Amaka will marry Izu.'

'Whether she likes it or not?' Ayo asked.

Yes, whether she likes it or not. I am your mother, and what I say is what you will do. Don't you have any sense? Didn't you hear him? Amaka, didn't you know he was a priest of God when you slept with him? He was only good as

140

a lover, as a man who arranged contracts for you, and not good enough to be your husband? I thought you used to spend your money on foolish men who deceived you. Now this man has given you such lovely boys and you have the guts to say, "I will not marry him". You will marry him. He has left the priesthood for your sake. You will not disappoint him. You will ruin him, and I will not stand by and let my daughter ruin such a good man. Where is that driver? Has he come?'

'I have my car. I can take you wherever you want to go,' said Ayo, who knew her mother better than Amaka did. Their mother would carry out the threat even if Izu changed his mind.

'Then take me to Izu's house.'

'Mother!'

'I say take me to his house. You heard me. I didn't have water in my mouth when I spoke to you. To Izu's house, or do you want me to take a taxi?'

'Mother, please sit down and let's get our bearings correct before we take a false step.'

'Are you taking me or not? You know I can hire a car. Are you bluffing?'

Ayo smiled in spite of the seriousness of the whole thing. As for Amaka, she said nothing. Nanny was somewhere in the kitchen. She heard everything but pretended not to hear.

'I am going to show you that I am your mother and that you do what I say, because what I say is the right thing at all times. I never make mistakes.' And with this, she got herself into the back seat of her daughter's car, and planted herself very solidly there.

'You want to make me your driver?' Ayo said, trying to release the tension a bit.

'You never know when one is serious. Go on, start your car.'

'I wonder whether they will let us in this early in the

141

morning,' said Ayo.

'When I tell them that I am Amaka's mother? What are you talking about?'

Ayo drove on. She wondered what her mother was going to say to Izu. She felt for Amaka. But, come to think of it, she thought, Amaka could have a divorce if she fails in this marriage. Her mother was right in saying that she has everything to gain and nothing to lose. She understood Amaka's point of view, of course – the old adage that 'once bitten twice shy' was correct in Amaka's case. She could give it a try though, especially as this case was a very special one. Yet she had her doubts. The marriage was not going to work. She knew it, because Amaka was not going to work hard for it.

They had to announce their names at the gate, and then the watchman threw the gate open to them. It was done in such a way that Ayo could not help thinking that the gateman had been briefed. They were shown into the sitting room and sat down. Something pricked Ayo as she sat down. She felt around and discovered that it was an ear-ring. She quickly put it in her handbag.

'What is that?' Her mother's ever-watchful eye had caught the movement.

'Oh, just a match I was using to pick my ear.'

Then Izu came out of his bedroom and welcomed them heartily. He offered them drinks, and Amaka's mother said she wanted some schnapps.

'Mother,' he said in his sweet way, and that was the first time he had called her 'mother'.

'Ayo, my daughter, did you hear him? My son, you have called me mother. I am your mother, my son.'

'Mother, I have no schnapps. I live the life of a man without a wife, a bachelor's life as the English say.'

'All right, whisky will do, but schnapps is better.'

A new bottle of whisky was brought in on a tray by Izu

himself. Amaka's mother poured libations, implying that both families had been joined together already, and this pleased Izu very much. Like a well-brought up person, he waited for his would-be mother-in-law to start. Ayo sat glumly as if she was merely a spectator.

'When do you want to marry my daughter?' Ayo sat up. She was startled. Even Izu was taken-aback. But he wanted Amaka, he needed her. So he said: 'As soon as she agrees to marry me. We shall have the native ritual first then allow a reasonable time before the church ceremony. You know it all. We have to give people time to recover from their shock over Amaka and I. This is the society that we all belong to and we have to recognise the norm. So she has come round at last? I must thank you, Mother. I knew you would be on my side, and once I had you on my side, I knew all would be well.'

He went into the other room because the telephone rang, and when he came out Ayo and her mother were already standing, ready to leave.

'I shall come this evening,' Izu said. 'I am wanted in the office, otherwise we could have had breakfast together.'

Ayo said nothing to her mother until they reached Amaka's house. She was not in. Nanny and the twins were not in either. So Ayo drove her mother to her own house and there she saw the message left by Amaka. She had taken off to Onitsha to see about the building. She would be away for a week. The key to the house was with her maid.

'Then, in that case, drive me to the airport,' said Amaka's mother.

'Don't you want to get home first?'

'What for? I have my money with me. I am not going home.'

She was driven to the airport. Ayo said nothing. For one thing, she knew that Amaka had not gone to Onitsha. Amaka was in Lagos. She did not know where exactly, but she was in Lagos.

143

'Buy the ticket then!' her mother shouted.

Ayo went meekly and bought a single ticket to Benin. She gave her fifty naira for the taxi fare, and prayed that the flight would not be cancelled.

'Amaka thinks she is clever. I am going to tell her that I am cleverer,' she said. Ayo said nothing. She was preoccupied with her own thoughts. The ear-ring? Whose was it? No, she should not behave in that way. After all, girls and ladies, mothers and grandmothers had visited Izu when he was just a priest. Now that he was a Federal Commissioner, he would receive more visitors. Then the thought hit her. It was more like a revelation than a thought. Just as their mother was fighting tooth and nail to have Amaka marry Izu, so were all mothers who knew Izu fighting tooth and nail to marry their daughters to him if they could. It was a matter of competition. Their mother was the first to realise this fact. Izu had gone high in the marriage market, with his youth, his position, his charm, and now 'defrocked' so to say, he would have no peace. The sooner he got married the better. The girls would continue to plague him, but at least her own sister would be the first in the queue. Anything could happen afterwards. And . . . The flight was announced.

'That's your flight, Mother.' She nudged her mother. She got up.

'Let's go,' she said.

'Go where?' Ayo asked in desperation.

'To your home,' she said.

'Aren't you travelling any more?'

'No.' And she was very serious.

'And you made me spend my money to buy you a ticket and . . .'

'I have not used it.'

'You have the boarding pass.'

'Which cannot be returned? Enough of your jesting. I am not travelling any more.'

144

'Can I have my fifty naira back? It's all I had in my handbag.'

'When we get home.'

Chapter 13

Ayo went to her home first, got lunch ready and made her mother eat. Surprisingly enough, she ate very well.

When she was resting, Ayo went to a neighbour and phoned Amaka's house. The nanny answered the phone, and said Amaka was sleeping.

'Tell her I'm coming right now. I will be there in fifteen minutes.'

She dashed out, hailed a taxi and went straight to Amaka's house. It was Nanny who paid the driver. Ayo knew that if she went back to the house for her handbag, her mother would suspect and jump into her car before she had time or the guts to stop her.

Amaka listened to Ayo very patiently as she narrated all the events of the day.

'Ayo,' she said in tears. 'I realised I had nowhere to go in Lagos except to you. Can you believe me? Isn't it strange? I wanted to hide, but there was nowhere to hide. I have nobody but you in Lagos. Adaobi, you know, cannot get over Izu and I, so I couldn't go to her. So we wandered around, did some shopping and, when we were tired, we came home. What am I going to do, Ayo?'

'Marry Izu.'

'Marry Izu?'

'Yes, marry him. Mother knows best. Don't throw away this golden opportunity. It comes once in a lifetime.'

'You know I don't love him.'

'I know, but marry him. Love will perhaps come later on.'

146

'And if it does not come?'

'You have nothing to lose. You have your twins. Didn't you hear Mother when she told us about our father?'

'Did you believe her?'

'Didn't you?' asked Ayo, surprised.

'I heard a different story.'

'From what quarter?'

'Of course. You are right that what you hear depends on the source,' Amaka said. She went on, 'It does not matter whether what she told us was true or not, a lot should be learnt from what she said.'

Ayo did not tell her about the ear-ring. It would weaken her case. So together they drove back to Ayo's house and got their mother round to Amaka's house. If she was surprised at seeing Amaka, she did not comment. She was still in her fighting mood. She demanded supper as if she had not eaten anything since morning and Nanny prepared food quickly.

Izu was about two hours late in coming. He had a case of schnapps in the boot of his car and asked Amaka's driver to go and fetch it. He knew how to impress his would-be mother-in-law already. She embraced Izu and was cheerful almost immediately. There was no beating about the bush.

'Amaka, when would be convenient for you and Izu to travel home?'

'Mother,' Amaka said, but quietly this time.

'Let's talk inside first,' Ayo said.

'We are not whispering anything inside. All has been said already.'

'It would appear that you are selling me to Izu, Mother. Why the hurry?'

'Meaning that I was responsible for your meeting Izu in the first place, that I spread the mat on which you and Izu slept and conceived the twins.'

Amaka and Ayo were so embarrassed at their mother's

language that they said nothing again.

'Children of these days fail to grab an opportunity when it presents itself. Amaka is one of them. But, Izu, don't worry, don't mind her behaviour. She really had a rough time. You will treat her well. And let me warn you that if you don't, if you leave her and run after other girls in Lagos, I am going to make trouble. I can make trouble, and I can make peace as well.

'We shall go home next week to tell Amaka's relatives. You should tell your own as well. Then in the middle of the month, let's say the second Sunday of next month, we shall expect you. You need a wife. A man in your position needs a good wife, to live a good life and ward off temptations.'

She called Nanny, who brought some glasses. She took a bottle of schnapps, opened it, and poured libations. She drank and gave Izu a drink.

'Give some to your wife,' she said, laughing.' Then she drank again and again, until her daughters thought she was going to get drunk and persuaded her to go to the bedroom, which she agreed to without a fuss.

Izu went home the next morning to arrange to go to Amaka's home. Amaka's mother went back home to spread the good news that the father of Amaka's twins was coming to perform the marriage rites. Everybody heard the news. Some members of the Cash Madam Club did not very much like the impending marriage and said so openly. Ayo accused them of jealousy and asked them whether they would honestly throw away that kind of fortune if it came their way.

Amaka was the only one who was indifferent to the whole thing. She took it stoically and refused even to discuss it with Ayo. Nanny had the courage one day to tell her mistress humbly but firmly that she did not have to marry the priest.

'If you don't feel like it, don't do it,' she said. 'I am much older than you are, and know how you feel. So I can see you do not want him as a husband. Don't let your mother push you into this kind of marriage.' Amaka thanked Nanny, but made no comment.

The twins were growing and looking more like their father every day. Amaka's business was thriving beyond her expectations. What did she want in marriage with Izu? Every day, something told her that the marriage would not take place let alone work. It was a strange feeling which she could not explain. The feeling was there night and day and nagged her. It affected Izu, who was getting impatient about the way Amaka felt towards him. He was exasperated when Amaka said that the journey to her home for the marriage rites had been postponed indefinitely. That night, Izu went away in anger and got himself drunk at a house party. Quite unconscious of what he was doing, he allowed a lady to take him home after the party and spent the night with her. He was alarmed in the morning when he woke up and saw her. He did not even recognise her, and he was visibly shocked. But the lady was unruffled and smiled at him. She had nothing on except a pair of ear-rings and a gold chain.

'This is my house,' the lady said.

'It was then that Izu realised that he was not in his own house.

'However, don't worry. I shall have breakfast ready in five minutes,' she said and disappeared into another room.

Izu looked around. He saw his trousers on the floor, put them on and grabbed his shirt. His hands were shaking as he dressed. He quickly dashed out of the house, hailed a taxi and jumped in. 'Ikoyi,' he said as the taxi driver looked enquiringly at him.

'Yes, I'll tell you when we get there.'

They drove on and on, until Izu realised that they were not going towards Ikoyi at all.

'Where are we going?' His voice shook a little and he saw

149

that his hands were also shaking. He tried to control himself. This was it. He was in the hands of armed robbers. It was then that he realised that the taxi driver was not alone. There was somebody with him in front. He had not seen him when he entered the taxi. The driver did not even reply to his question. He and the other man began to talk. Izu did not understand them. It was still early. He looked at his wrist, but his watch was not there. He must have left it at the lady's house. It must be about six in the morning. But where was he?

Then, all of a sudden, he saw a bus speeding towards them very fast. The driver and his companion shouted, he raised his hands and that was all he could remember when he woke up in a hospital bed.

He did not know how long he had been there when he saw the Bishop at his bedside. The Bishop was holding his hand and talking to him as a father would talk to his son.

'You will be all right, my son,' the Bishop said to him. 'You were lucky. The other occupants of the taxi died before they got to the hospital. You suffered only from shock. There was no internal bleeding. The X-ray shows a twisted arm which will be all right in due course. I am so sorry, my child.'

As luck would have it, after the accident occured, the first people to arrive at the scene were two nuns and their driver who were driving into Lagos from Ikorodu. With the help of the driver, the nuns carried Izu and the other two into their own vehicle and raced to the hospital. On identifying him, they got in touch with the Bishop at once.

When the Bishop left, Izu was deep in thought. Was his miraculous escape from death a divine intervention? Had he sinned by abandoning the Church that brought him up by hand, that saved his life and made him what he was? It was a mortal sin. Where was Amaka? Had she heard of his escape from death? Had she come to see him and was not allowed to do so? What happened before the accident?

Who was the lady he spent the night with? Why did Amaka postpone indefinitely the journey to her home for the marriage rites? Why was she behaving in this way? Did she actually want to marry him? She did not want to. She had said that several times to him. It was he who had persisted. Would he have proposed marriage if it was not for the twins? The answer was no. He would not have. And the sin was committed anyway. It was one and the same thing. There were three lives involved, Amaka's and the twins'! There was no turning back now. He could decide not to go on but what about the twins? Would they grow up not knowing who their father was?

And why was he so upset that he got himself drunk and was taken home by a lady he did not know? Did anybody plan this? Who planned it and for what purpose? He was shocked at himself. He was much happier before he met Amaka. Now he was not only unhappy but restless, worldly and a sinner. Girls, together with their mothers, had tempted him. In some cases, he had succumbed to their temptations. Would this sort of thing continue after his marriage to Amaka? He had made a mess of his life. What was he going to do?

Amaka received a telephone call from a nun one morning. She had recently returned from her home. She had gone to tell her mother that the date for the marriage ceremonies had been postponed indefinitely. Her mother was so angry that she called her all sorts of names openly. Somehow, she was not touched by what her mother said to her. She remained at home to see to the completion of her house and made one or two quick deals before she returned to Lagos. Nanny had told her that Izu did not telephone and had not called to see them. Ayo had come to see how they were getting on and had gone to Cotounu to buy some materials for their trip to the East.

Amaka telephone Ayo to tell her she was back and Ayo said she was coming over to see her. She was with her when the nun called.

'Amaka speaking.' She covered the telephone and asked Ayo to come near.

'Yes, you can come any day. I have returned from home only yesterday . . . Yes, Thursday afternoon would do. At four o'clock . . . But I can come over. Do you have transport? . . . All right. Four then. Thank you.'

She hung up, and looked at Ayo questioningly.

'An Irish nun. She did not give her name. She wants to see me. Something has happened to Izu.' Amaka held her sister tight.

Ayo telephoned Izu's home but there was no reply. She telephoned the office and was told that the Hon. Commissioner had gone on a tour of Europe with the Head of State.

'How did he take the postponement of the marriage ceremonies?' Ayo asked her sister.

'Very badly.'

'And the next day, you travelled home.'

'Yes.'

'And you were away for two weeks. A lot could happen in two weeks. Let's wait for the nun. She said Thursday?'

'Yes, Thursday at four o'clock. You heard nothing, Ayo?'

'Nothing. I was busy.'

'Of course.'

'We can do nothing until the nun comes. Today is Tuesday.'

'Stay with us. Don't go home. I am frightened,' Amaka pleaded.

Thursday came at last. At four o'clock the Irish nun drove in. Ayo greeted her. She came alone. Tea was served and she chattered away cheerfully. Then Amaka came in and greeted her too. The twins were brought in by Nanny and the Irish

152

nun gazed at them. She could not hide her interest in the twins.

'Come, my darlings,' she said to them. 'I am Sister Maria Angela from your father's parish. Come and say hello to Sister.'

Amaka and Ayo watched their mouths open wide. This was the first introduction by the nun, who went on: 'And how would you like Sister Maria Angela to take you to Dublin for Christmas?'

'Sister Maria Angela,' Ayo said, quite in control of herself. 'You are not behaving like a Sister of God. Just tell my sister why you have come to see her, or get out.'

The nun was taken aback. 'Oh, I am so terribly sorry. They are such lovely twins. And Father Mclaid was a twin himself, so there is no mistaking the fact. And . . .' She stopped as Ayo got up.

'His name is Izu. We call him Izu in this house. He is no longer a Reverend Father. The Bishop granted him dispensation a long time ago and he is going to marry my sister very soon. And, as you already know, the twins are his and my sister's.'

'Oh, I am so terribly sorry,' said the nun and took a sip of the tea. Amaka served her some cakes. She wasn't angry. She was not upset. Izu was alive. If he was dead, the nun would have said it outright. But she wanted to be sure, so she asked:

'Before you go on, Sister Maria Angela, is it true that the Commissioner has gone abroad with the Head of State? You see, we got this information from the Ministry, and there was no way of confirming it before you came.'

'Yes and no,' Sister Maria Angela said.

'Izu is alive and well?'

'Yes, Father Mclaid is alive and well.'

'Thank God for that. Izu and Mclaid are one and the same person,' Amaka said, almost laughing aloud. 'Now you can say what you want to say. I am prepared to listen to you.'

153

Ayo was fuming. Amaka was relaxed. Nanny was quiet as usual. The twins were playing. The nun drank her tea and went on.

'The Bishop sent me. Father Mclaid has gone back to the Chu ch. You see, his dispensation had not been made public. So, when he confessed all to the Bishop, the Bishop took him back into the fold. I was detailed to come and give you the news. You may ask when all this took place. I am prepared to tell you. Father Mclaid had an accident, the morning after you postponed the journey to your home. Miraculously, he did not die. The two other people in the taxi died. And Father Mclaid thought his narrow escape from death was due to divine intervention. We all think so too. So he went to the Bishop and. . .'

'Ayo, Nanny, didn't I tell you? Sister Maria Angela, thank you.' Amaka was talking very excitedly, and it was the nun who was surprised at the turn of events.

'We must celebrate this and . . .'

'Stop it, Amaka. Sister Maria Angela, where is Izu now?' Ayo asked.

'With the Bishop. His penance is not very severe. He is so well liked by all of us.'

Ayo shouted: 'When you get back to the nunnery or whatever you call it, tell Izu that I will confront him with my mother in a very short time and that . . .'

She was interrupted by Amaka. 'Tell Izu,' she said, 'that I would like to see him and thank him for this noble decision, and that I was the first to know that there would be no marriage. And finally, that I shall forever remain grateful to him for proving to the world that I am a mother as well as a woman.'